Changelings

Book1

Dragons and Demons

James A. McVean
MCVEANJIM@aol.com

James A. McVean

Changelings Book 1 – Dragons and Demons

Changelings
Dragons and Demons

<u>Dedications and Acknowledgements</u>

This book is primarily dedicated to Nicola and Freya, my lovely wife and daughter

*

A huge thank you to A.A.Attanasio a true earthbound Fire Lord, for his inspirational kick that drove me to decide to publish this book – Cheers AL

*

Also cheers to the Lads in Flotta, my real job, where I got the time to write this book on those long Orkney nights…

*

Finally many thanks to Ruth for her reading, encouragement and fantastically helpful reviews of this book in the *GetWriting* days.

Contents

Chapter 1

Jack the Hawk

The lad moved slowly down the narrow cobbled street, avoiding eye contact and exchanging no pleasantries with passers-by. He wanted to blend in, to become unnoticed, and dressed as he was in a filthy grey tunic and shabby brown breeks, he succeeded easily.

The sun was warm and the sky was clear, yet he stuck to the shadows, slipping stealthily into a narrow lane between the high wooden buildings. The thatched roofs almost touched above him and the thin line of daylight did little to dispel the gloom, as he wended his way past the Dragon's Head Inn towards his workplace.

The city square was busy, stalls and carts thronged with vendors and customers. Farmers sold their wares to merchants and left with pouches and purses bulging with silver and gold. It was market-day, busiest of the week; rich pickings for a careful pickpocket.

His nickname was the Hawk - Jack the Hawk - well known amongst the lowlifes and thieves of Ness. A small city with an equally small castle and a crumbling defensive wall that had been built centuries before, to keep out an enemy that no longer existed. Nonetheless it prospered on the main trade route between the capital - Darkhaven and the distant Western city states of Grimswade and Haarsfalt.

Jack picked up a small, empty beer-keg and carried it on his shoulder through the crowds, before setting it down and settling for work.

He sat on the small barrel, eyes closed, chewing on a long sweet blade of grass. The shoppers took no notice of the lad, dressed in rags, relaxing in the sun. Some brushed by roughly, annoyed at the inconvenience of having to walk around him, and they paid the price.

Jack's small blade would slash swiftly out and cut the strings holding their money pouches and his nimble fingers darted into his loose tunic with his rewards. He had been caught red handed a couple of times, usually by his victim or spotted by another, he had even been chased by the city guard, but never caught. Jack knew the penalty for thievery, he faced a terrible flogging and a lengthy term in the local jail, this made him learn his trade very carefully and become one of the best in his field.

"Mornin' Hawk lad." The familiar drawl of Harry the Crow filled his senses as he blocked out the warm sunshine.

The telltale aroma of Crow's unwashed flesh and rotting teeth announced his presence louder and clearer than the tower bell that had sounded at noon. Jack's guts twisted and his heart skipped a beat. He wiped his sweaty palms on his legs..

"Wotcha got fur me t'day boy?"

Jack opened his eyes and looked up at the gaunt man hovering over him like a dark phantom. He wore a filthy black jacket and an ill fitting pair of baggy breeks, tied at the waist with an old rope. He had hair like black straw, and if he stood still you might mistake him for a scarecrow. Some said that the rope around his waist was the same that the city guard had used when Harry had swung on the gallows for murder; the livid red scar around his throat was testament to the truth of the rumour. But he had survived, and once he had paid the price for his crime he was freed. In no time he became legend among the city's lowlifes and cut-throats, their self-styled leader and divider of the take.

Taking care to breath only through his mouth, Jack smiled cautiously and reached into his shirt and produced two small purses of coin.

"And the rest!" Crow growled threateningly.

Jack heaved a theatrical sigh and produced two more pouches. Crow snatched them with a greedy glint in his one good eye, then he disappeared into the crowd, his dark coat billowing.

"Ha! Got one over you! You old sod!" Jack called under his breath, the one remaining purse - the heaviest – was safely tucked down his breeks.

Jack left the hustle and bustle of the marketplace and wandered over to the fountain and sat on the edge, leaning over to sip from the clear, cool waters. He slaked his thirst and gazed at his reflection, shadowy and distorted, framed by the fluffy white clouds floating high above.

He sat daydreaming; thinking of taking his stash of coins and escaping this gloomy city and travelling to the distant capital with its fabulous towers and shining walls.

His money was safe in the hills, buried in the back of a deep dark cave. Local legends told of how it had once been a dragons lair, and superstitious fear kept everyone away. It was probably the safest place in all the land.

He was deep in his reverie when an old man stepped up to take a drink.

"Ah, that's better!" his deep voice rumbled, wiping his face with his baggy cloak sleeve.

Jack was more than a little annoyed with the company and he scowled at his uninvited guest.

The old man had bushy white eyebrows that met above his large hooked nose and piercing eyes of the deepest crystal-blue that seemed to penetrate deep into his soul. His ruddy cheeks were almost hidden by a thick beard that cascaded over his large chest, but the dome of his head was completely hairless and to Jack it appeared shaven.

Who is this stranger? Jack thought.

"I am Belthor, a travelling mage, and druid of the White Goddess Danu," The man answered his unasked question, in a jolly and surprisingly deep voice.

"You are no mage, look at you!" Jack burst out laughing, "Everyone knows mages wear fancy clothes and live in fantastic magical castles!"

7

"Oh do they?" he frowned, "and just how many wizards have you encountered my young friend?"

Jack smiled, "None, you are the first, if indeed you are really one! But," he added with a laugh, "I have heard plenty of minstrel songs and fireside tales in the tavern!"

Belthor chuckled good-naturedly, "Do not be so quick to judge people by their outward appearances young hawk, for you would appear a fine young lad and not the cut-purse you really are."

Jack blinked, swallowed and looked around to see if anyone had overheard his comment.

"Don't worry Jack, I will not run to the guard. And you need not think to stab me with that tiny knife either." Belthor warned in a firm tone, "I can see the good in you lad, you shine with an energy that I have seldom seen in one so young."

"Shine? Me?" Jack laughed nervously, looking down at his dirty nails.

Belthor set his staff against the wall, and placed his pack on the ground, opened it and pulled out a roll of cloth. He shook it in the bright afternoon sunlight, the amazing multi-coloured pattern was breathtaking. Jack had never seen such a fine cloth, it would have easily fetch twenty gold pieces in the auctions.

Belthor spread the cloth on the dusty ground and knelt in the centre, the whole thing was covered in an endless knot that seemed to swirl and twist with every colour of the rainbow, staring too long made Jack dizzy, but it also stirred something deep inside him.

"Jack, would you watch my bag for a moment? I have an important matter to take care of."

Jack nodded, expecting Belthor to leave. Instead he lay flat and closed his eyes.

Time passed, the moment stretching.

Jack frowned and as he waited, he studied the worn leather pack, the sunlight glinted on a small sliver flask resting in plain view. Temptation got the better of him and he slipped the shining container into his pocket.

Moments later Belthor opened his eyes and whispered sharply, "Lailoken!" He sat bolt upright, tears were running down his cheeks into his snowy beard.

Jack crouched by the old man and placed a hand on his shoulder, "What is it Belthor?" he asked gently.

Belthor shook his head slightly, "Forgive my foolish show of emotion, Jack. A good friend of mine has just been captured...and we are all at terrible risk."

"Captured? How? Where?" Jack was mystified.

Belthor sighed and rose shakily to his feet, "I am sorry young Hawk, I have said too much already. I must make haste. Take good care Jack."

Panic gripped Jack's heart, though he did not know why, "Where are you going Belthor?"

The old wizard smiled sadly, "East Jack, homewards. My skills will be desperately needed."

Before Jack could ask another question, Belthor packed the cloth and disappeared into the crowds

Jack sat heavily on the rim of the fountain, his head reeled, filled with flights of fancy. He pictured himself racing after the wizard and offering his help, to overcome the desperate peril that he and his friends faced. But his common-sense got the better of him, and his growling stomach told him the afternoon was wearing on, so he made his way to the inn.

*

The Dragon's Head Inn was busy, but not so busy that they would dream of turning away paying custom. The huge Innkeeper, George, wore a filthy apron, his round belly was covered in grease and soot but he cooked the best steak pie in the city, and a silver crown got Jack the best of fare the Inn could provide.

He ate his fill, and even drank two foaming tankards of warm ale, straining the bits through his teeth. A minstrel entertained the drunken farmers and their families, he sang and then played his flute and the room hushed as he created a beautiful tune. Jack sat and listened with eyes closed, feeling sleepy with his full satisfied stomach, he placed his palms on his thighs and lost himself, drifting happily on the tune.

Suddenly he remembered the silver flask he had *borrowed* from Belthor. He pulled it from his pocket and examined it closely; the container was beautifully engraved with a Dragon on the wing. Jack's eyes were drawn to the crude painting hanging on the far wall; a huge black knight stood with one foot resting on the snout of a dead dragon. He felt angered by the picture, which was strange, for he had seen it dozens of times before.

The flask in his hand began to feel warm, and to Jack's amazement it began to glow softly, so he hastily stuffed it back into his pocket and headed out into the cool night air. The streets were busy even though the sun had set an hour ago, so Jack ducked into the alley behind the Inn, melting unseen into the shadows.

He removed the flask again, and was slightly disappointed to find the glow had gone, and it was cool to the touch.

Was that just the firelight reflecting on the silver, or did it really give off a light? He thought.

Jack pulled the cork, sniffing at the contents very carefully. His nostrils were delighted by the sweet aroma of the liquid inside. He tipped the container very slightly, letting one drip land on his finger, then with one moments hesitation, he stuck his finger into his mouth.

Jack's tongue began to tingle slightly and his head spun, wonderful feelings flooded through him. No hesitation this time, he put it to his lips and took two gulps, before replacing the cork stopper.

Seconds later his head began to spin terribly and a feeling of dire dread swept through him, as wave after wave of hot agony lanced though his stomach. He cried with the pain, and to his horror smoke began to belch from between his lips. Jack screamed and a gout of flame leapt from his mouth, igniting a pile of rubbish. Terror filled him now, his senses reeled, something terrible was happening and he was powerless to stop it.

He ran from the alley, down the street, smoke still billowing though his gritted teeth and tears stinging his eyes. Jack fled through the night, small spouts of flames escaping him in bursts as he ran. He stumbled in blind panic till he almost fell into the fountain, kneeling down he thrust his head into the water. Gulp after gulp cascaded down his throat, cooling and quenching the fire burning in his stomach.

He made his way out of the city, over the fields, through the forest and into the hills. His cave was dark and warm, straw covered the deepest corner; he often slept there, and he thought that this was the best place to come under these terrible circumstances.

He settled into the dry bedding, his head still spinning.

Why didn't I just leave the cursed bottle alone? He thought, deep regret filling him, sparking anger at himself and the wizard.

Suddenly his stomach began churning again, gurgling and boiling. Small flames burst forth lighting the darkness, almost setting fire to the bedding. Panic swept though him again, it seemed that emotions set off the fire.

Tears welled up, Jack's head pounded, and to make things worse he itched furiously all over. After hours of tossing and turning he finally drifted into a fitful, dreamless sleep.

Chapter 2

Fight and Flight

Morning sunlight flooded the cave. Squinting, Jack stretched thinking the previous day nothing but a terrible dream, until he completely opened his eyes. In the light he saw his bare arms were covered in scabs, cracked and sore, weeping clear fluid.

Jack screamed and flames scorched the jagged cave walls. He clenched his fists in fear, the scabs flaked and cracked further, and to his horror he could see something strange underneath. With a terrible curiosity he studied the back of his hand, picking at the scabs with shaking fingers. One particularly crunchy, brown sore fell from his hand, revealing tiny glistening scales of the brightest green.

Jack sat bolt-upright and suddenly realised that his entire body was scabbed over. A wave of dizziness swept over him, and he had to take several deep breaths and grip the wall for support. He would have to go after Belthor and beg his mercy.

He went into the dark of the cave and lifted a flat stone, below it the earth was soft and with a few moments digging, he uncovered a small chest. He retrieved a small silver key from a thin chain around his neck and unlocked the box. Inside was a stash of silver and gold coins, there was probably enough to keep him comfortably for the rest of his life; but being greedy, he always seemed to want 'just one more purse.'

Jack wore a scarf around his face and wrapped himself tightly within his cloak and filled a small pouch with gold, before he buried the box again, then headed into the city.

As he walked he was very self-conscious of the scabs on his legs and body crackling and flaking off. Luckily the itching passed quickly and now he had to go to the inn and buy some provisions. Passing through the streets with his hood pulled tight and no bare skin showing, Jack tried to blend in as much as possible. He followed the back-alleys and narrow lanes to the rear of the Inn. This was where he had first sipped from the flask, he shuddered at his own stupidity.

He tapped at the backdoor with his gloved hand, setting off a barking dog, and waited till George appeared at the upstairs window.

"Wotcha want at this ungodly hour?" He growled harshly.

Jack reached into his pouch and pulled out a piece of gold, and in an extravagant gesture he tossed it up to the man hanging out of the window. His huge fist snapped out and swiped the piece as it passed. His face lit up and eyes widened as he realised what he held.

"Oh forgive me stranger, I do not usually rise so early in the day." He stumbled through an apology, disappearing inside only to appear at the door moments later, wearing a pair of slippers and a well worn night-shirt.

"Come in stranger, come in please!" He beckoned Jack into the bar.

"George, its me. Jack. Jack the Hawk!" He spoke through the muffled cloth.

"Jack? What on earth?" confusion etched his face, "What the hell's the get-up for?"

"Don't ask George!" Jack dismissed.

George's eyes widened in fear, "No! Not the plague!" He blanched and backed off several steps.

"No not the plague, George. I just need to leave the town unnoticed, I've got to avoid certain people. But first I need some provisions for the journey. "

"Crow!" Triumph lit the landlord's eyes, " You want to get away…"

Jack silenced him with two more gold coins, pressed into his sweaty palms.

The Innkeep's eyes widened, he now had more than three months income in his hand. He closed his eyes and nodded, "My lips are sealed Jack!"

Jack gave the Innkeeper a list of provisions and items he required for his trip, and he scurried off to the kitchens. He returned with a small cloth sack, filled with travelling food.

Jack took the sack and left, thanking the innkeeper as he went. The market stalls were being assembled in the square, and early shoppers out and about. He moved quickly towards the east gate and was almost clear, when suddenly a figure dressed in filthy black barred his way.

"Where you headed Hawk?" Crow's voice was as cold as the grave, "You think you can leave without my eyes and ears knowing your every move?"

Crow pulled out a wicked looking, curved dagger, and began cleaning his finger nails, with an air of deadly menace.

"Harry...I...I was just coming to see you." Jack lied through his scarf.

Crow's face screwed into a snarl, "Look me in the eye when you lie to me boy!" he reached out and snatched at the scarf covering Jack's face.

But he quickly recoiled in horror, for Jack's face was a mass of splitting scabs, and his eyes had changed; they had turned bright yellow and the pupils were now slits.

Jack saw the fear in Crow's eyes and the old criminal took a backward pace.

"Demon!" Crow cried, slashing out with the knife.

Time seemed to slow down as the blade sliced through the air. Jack looked up at the light dancing slowly along its deadly, curved edge, and then his instincts took over. The blade swished through the air missing him by scant inches. Jack was amazed to find that he could move so quickly, easily avoiding the deadly weapon.

He leapt backwards, pulling off the cloak and gloves, more of the scabs had now fallen off, revealing perfect iridescent scales of pale green. His fingers were now tipped with razor sharp talons, each as deadly as Crow's weapon.

Cries of fear and horror sounded from the small crowd who had gathered to watch the unfolding drama before them. This distracted Jack momentarily and Crow took full advantage of this chance. He brought the blade down hard across Jack's shoulder, shredding the tunic but amazingly the dagger never pierced the scales, the weapon was deflected easily.

Jack retaliated swiping with his deadly claws, raking Crow across the face, cutting him deeply. Blood welled in four lines, and Crow howled in pain, clutching at his torn features. Fear fuelled Crow's rage and he quickly grabbed the lad by the throat, squeezing hard, then harder still. Jack desperately dug his talons into Crow's wrists, drawing blood as dark spots swam before his eyes. Crow loosened his grip enough for Jack to draw breath; this was his last mistake. Jack roared out a breath of fire, scorching his enemy and setting his straggly hair on fire.

Crow turned and fled, smouldering, into the growing crowd of terrified onlookers.

Jack stood for a moment catching his breath, adrenaline filling him with nervous energy. Then he became aware of the widening circle of spectators, every face told a story, they also told him his condition had further deteriorated.

"I think I'd better get out of here!" He thought aloud.

A piercing whistle sounded and the tramp of several booted men echoed at the far side of the square; the city guard were on their way. Jack grabbed his provisions and fled Eastwards, speeding across the tilled fields with seemingly boundless energy. The small group of guards gave a half-hearted chase, before giving up and returning to the city.

*

Jack was changing, his body was transforming and his senses were becoming sharper. His sight was amazingly detailed; he could pick out a tiny song bird in a tree over a mile distant and his hearing was similarly keen; every sound was crisp and clear.

Jack stopped by a small lake as the sun rose to its zenith. He ate a quick meal of bread and cheese, and knelt by the waters edge, bending to take a sip. The face that greeted him was not his own; his mouth was becoming wider; his nose was flattening and the nostrils widening. It was his eyes that scared him

15

the most; they had enlarged and turned a smoky yellow, with a pale blue slit for a pupil, topped with heavy lids and protruding bony ridges. It seemed that every inch of his skin was turning to the tiny green scales.

Jack pulled open his tunic; his chest and belly was covered with large segmented plates, thick and hard. He hunched forwards and rolled his shoulders; surprisingly the scales were very flexible and seemed to give him a far freer sense of movement in his joints.

Stripping off the remainder of his garments, he leapt into the lake. The cool, clear water cleaned the remaining scabs from his body and left him completely changed; no longer a human boy. He swam, luxuriating in the exercise and was so engrossed that he failed to notice the horseman riding across the grassland towards him.

The rider dismounted and began rummaging through Jack's belongings, picking out the valuables and food, tossing the clothing aside.

"Hey that's mine," Jack cried from a distance out in the water, swimming as fast as he could towards the shore, "Stop thief!"

The rider stood and looked out at the strange, green beast yelling and waving wildly. He knelt, seemingly unfazed, and filled his water bottle, before mounting his steed and galloping off into the hills.

Jack was furious as he leapt from the water and pulled on his clothes. Flames shot from his mouth as his anger grew. The rider was just cresting a distant hill, disappearing from view. He could not believe his bad luck, the flask was in his pouch and now the pouch was in the rider's saddlebag.

Jack sniffed the air, using his new-found senses, and found that he could follow the man's scent; it was as if he had left a colourful trail of pure smell. So off he set, at a fast run, across the plains and up over the hill. The land ahead was all rolling hills; thick forests and deep gullies; an intricate maze of hiding places and caves. To any normal man this would have meant that his search would be near impossible, but Jack was no longer normal.

By nightfall he had tracked the man to a cave, deep in the forest. Creeping stealthily into the valley, moving silently from tree to tree, he spied

16

the horse tied at the cave mouth. The thief was sitting on a tree stump by a small campfire, munching on *his* food. He was dressed in dark tan boots, and a heavy deep green cloak tied at the neck with a silver pin.

Jack climbed the nearest tree, and made his way along an overhanging branch. He dropped, landing silently behind his foe.

"Hello, my green friend." The man said, without turning, his voice deep and mellow.

That simple statement stole the wind from Jack's sails.

"Don't feel bad, I heard you miles back, though I was surprised you made it this far alone," he turned, a handsome dark eyed man with a broad frame and a tangle of long brown hair, shot through with streaks of silver, tied untidily at the nape of his neck.

"My things…give them back." Jack growled softly, tensing ready to fight if he had to.

The man chuckled and tossed Jack the pouch of money, the weight of the flask reassured him. Strangely he showed no sign of surprise at the appearance of the green lad before him.

"Sit and share some food with me friend." He commanded in a friendly manner.

Jack sat on a moss covered stone, without thinking twice about it. The stranger passed him a chunk of cheese and cut him a slice of bread.

"Thanks," Jack said, forgetting that it was his own food he was sharing, "What name do you go by stranger?"

"Lupin," Was his simple reply.

The man sat staring into the small flames of the fire, apparently deep in thought. Jack ate, studying the stranger before him; in the fire light he saw a ring glinting on the man's finger, it was ornately engraved with a dragon, similar to the one on the wizard's flask.

Lupin caught Jack's gaze, and quickly covered his hand.

"Do you know a wizard called Belthor?" Jack asked.

Lupin whipped around instantly, "Belthor? Yes I do know him, what has happened to him?...Quickly boy, spit it out!" he snapped.

"I...I, he was in our market this afternoon." Jack blurted out.

"And!"

"He sort of placed a mat on the ground and closed his eyes for a while, then told me his friend had been captured..."

Lupin frowned, raising a large hand stopping him, "Captured?"

Jack nodded, "He said the name Lailoken too."

"Then it has begun..." He heaved a deep sigh, "I though we had a few more weeks..." Lupin muttered quietly to himself.

"I took a silver flask from him, and...and he turned me into this!" Jack cried.

Lupin smiled sadly, shaking his head, "No my friend, you are mistaken. You alone control your own destiny."

Jack frowned, confused.

"Belthor merely set the wheels of change in motion. You have always been a Changeling."

"A Changeling?"

Lupin laughed, a deep resonant sound, "It seems a demonstration is required."

He stood and removed his ring, then unbuttoned his shirt, and to Jack's astonishment, stripped till he was naked. He stood facing the fire, bathed half in the flickering, orange glow and half in the light of the full moon.

"Mighty Mother, Sister moon, hidden Father, bring the change upon your Son!"

Lupin hunched forward, loud cracks filled the air, bones snapped and reformed, course black hair grew rapidly. He collapsed on to all fours, his face distorted and seemed to stretch, he screamed terribly and long fangs forced their way through his gums.

Jack's heart beat in his throat, excitement and fear churned in his stomach. The mysterious stranger transformed into a huge, black wolf, right before his eyes.

Lupin looked up at the moon, and let out a mournful howl. Immediately answering cries filled the distance, from all directions. Jack turned and glanced into the gloom, fearful. Lupin turned to face him, standing five foot at the shoulder, gazing almost level into his large, lime-green eyes. He could feel the peace in the heart of the huge animal, as their minds linked telepathically, Lupin's familiar voice echoing in his head.

"So now you see my true form, and you, young Jack, are half way to becoming your own true self. Drink the remainder of Belthor's flask, and the hidden pathways in your memory shall be completely re-opened."

"What's in the flask?" Jack asked nervously, pulling the silver flask from his pouch, forgetting that he had not even mentioned his own name.

"I am not sure, but I think it is the tears of a newly hatched Dragon. They are very magical beasts indeed." Lupin explained, "But now I will leave you to do what you think is right, I will await your answer in one hour atop a nearby hill."

At that, Lupin turned and bounded off silently into the darkness, leaving Jack to think.

"Me? A Changeling?" Jack whispered to himself, a thousand questions whirled around in his head.

He sat by the fire and heaved a sigh, and stared at the silver engraved dragon in the palm of his green hand. It was too late to turn back, so he pulled the cork and downed the remaining fluid from the flask. A strange buzzing filled his head, he stood and staggered slightly, dizzy with the new knowledge zooming around his brain.

Strangely, he suddenly knew the chant at the very moment he began to speak, beginning a whisper and ending a scream. Each word tasted different in his mouth, his voice deepened and throat rumbled with each uttered syllable.

"Dragon Fly... Dragon Eye... Dragon Be...DRAGON ME!"

The forest grew silent, birds and insects stilled their night-songs, as if they knew something fantastic was happening.

Bones snapped, elongated, grew and thickened. Pain lanced through his young body, flames flew from his throat as his scream changed into a roar. The shirt split as his back broadened and a pair of huge wings began to grow magically from his shoulders, the pain became unbearable and Jack collapsed onto his belly, slipping into unconsciousness.

*

Awaking moments later, Jack lifted his long neck and flexed his new muscles. In the mouth of the cave, Lupin's horse whinnied and reared in fright.

Jack turned and looked at the poor tethered animal, "Don't worry, I won't eat you." He soothed the animal.

The horse settled, understanding him.

Jack sat on his haunches and examined himself, marvelling at his new body, from his huge leathery wings, long spiny tail and huge pale green translucent chest plates. He looked over his shoulder using an amazingly long flexible neck, all across his back were countless small dark green scales, rippling with the new-found muscles beneath.

A giddy excitement swept over him, "I am going to fly!" He cried into the night.

Jack flexed his huge wings, flapping them rhythmically, and slowly he left the ground, the art of flying seemed to come like some sort of second nature to him. In a few moments he was swooping and diving, climbing and banking, gliding and soaring through the night sky.

He had dreamt of this for years, now he knew the truth of Lupin's words.

Jack let out a roar of sheer joy, the sense of freedom was unbelievable. For the first time in his life he felt at one with himself, this was where he truly belonged.

Chapter 3

Wolf and Man

After several minutes of fun filled flight, Jack remembered that he had to meet Lupin waiting on the hilltop. He cast his new eyes over the hills, the normally green grass appeared silvery grey; shining in the moonlight. With two flaps of his leathery wings, he plunged into a steep dive, crying out telepathically, "LUPIN, HERE I COME!"

Jack landed with a thump that shook the hillside, delighted with his new-found flying ability. Lupin padded silently out of the shadows between the trees his shaggy head held low to the ground, Jack instinctively knew he was annoyed.

"Every creature within a hundred leagues will have heard that cry Dragon!" Lupin growled with a low rumble.

Ashamed, Jack lowered his head to the grass, exhaling a deep snuffling breath, that ruffled Lupin's fur, "I'm sorry Lupin, I was just so excited."

Lupin nodded to a pile of deadwood, "Could you try and light this Jack?"

Jack took a deep breath and exhaled over the dry wood; a waft of hot air blasted from his throat. Lupin sat and waited patiently, his head cocked to the side the way only dogs can.

Jack growled, angry at himself; he noticed that something tightened in his stomach as the frustration took hold. Tensing his new muscles, he took another breath and roared flames over the wood, scorching a huge area of the grass behind it too. Lupin leapt clear as Jack reared up and roared in triumph.

"Settle Jack, I have something important to tell you."

"Wait…" Jack's scaly brows crinkled into a frown, "How do you know my name? I have never mentioned it before."

Lupin sighed, then with a mental chuckle, "Jack please, I will explain everything, please be patient."

Jack narrowed his eyes in suspicion, but took a deep breath and did as he was bidden.

"Jack, you have been watched continuously, from the day you were left on the steps of the temple, to your amazing fight with Harry the Crow this very morning."

Jack blinked and shook his head slowly, "What…"

Lupin continued, cutting off Jack's question, "Belthor deliberately sought you out Jack; he knew the time was right and the temptation to take the flask would be beyond you, and now you sit here in your true form."

Once again Jack shook his head in disbelief. There was no doubting his present condition, but to have been watched all his life. He did not really believe it.

"I can see that you don't really believe this yet Jack, and I think that you will find this next revelation even harder to swallow. You are the *Chosen one* Jack, prophesied in ancient times to lead the light from the darkness. Please trust me Jack, I have something very important to do. Be patient, all will become clearer in time."

Lupin's words echoed in Jack's whirling mind, as a thousand and one questions fought for his attention.

Lupin sat and arched his back, giving a long, high howl. It echoed around the hill and the surrounding forests. Moments later several wolves answered with individual cries of their own. Jack raised his long neck and head, sniffing the air, sensing movement in the forests skirting the hillside.

Even in his dragon form Jack felt uneasy; like most humans he had been led to believe that wolves were vicious and deadly; though the truth of the matter was that nobody from his town had ever been attacked in living memory. Yet the city council still paid a silver crown for each and every pelt delivered to its doors.

Long before they were visible to the naked eye, Jack spotted the silver moonlight reflected in the eyes of dozens of wolves climbing the hill. Low growls and whines filled the quiet night, and one large white wolf crept cautiously from the shadows.

"Brother, Do not fear this Dragon," Lupin communicated with the wolf, "He is here at my request."

The wolf sniffed warily at Jack's huge foot. "Forgive me Dragon, but you are the first of your kind that I have encountered."

Jack gave the wolf a delighted toothy grin, "Don't worry wolf, for you are the first wolf I have met too!"

Slowly the clearing filled as the rest of the reassured animals melted into view. Dozens of wolves filled the clearing, the dominant males at the fore, she-wolves and pups at a discreet and respectful distance. The young yapped and yelped, never having been in such a large pack, and even more so at the sight of the huge, scaly, green dragon with the large yellow eyes.

Lupin leapt onto a large rock, barking loudly, silencing the gathered canine throng.

"Brothers and Sisters, something bad is happening in our world. A great evil has crossed from the eternal darkness into our light."

Complete silence greeted his opening words.

"It devours everything and will not rest till all its brethren are free to turn this world to ashes."

This sent all the wolves barking and yapping in fear and anger. Lupin let them show their astonished anger before addressing them again, "Brothers and Sisters, we must help stop this."

"Help?" said the white wolf, "Help how? And who?"

Jack looked down on the gathering, wondering just what this evil thing was that Lupin spoke of.

"All animal kind, white one, including…humans." said Lupin

All the wolves fell silent, each stared intently at the white wolf; their leader. He looked up at the moon and howled long and hard.

"Mother!" he cried at the moon in anguish, "Mother! Please help us to forgive the mankind. Forgive them the hunting. Forgive them the killing. Help us to help them fight this scourge."

All the wolves began to howl, a terrible sound of deep sadness, tinged with a furious wild rage.

Caught up in the emotion Jack also roared into the night, ashamed to think of the rich merchant's wives with their wolf fur trimmed cloaks, he actually felt ashamed to be partly human.

Several long moments passed before silence once again descended.

"We will need you to track and harry these despicable monsters, become the eyes and ears of our forces, but not the teeth!"

A few of the males growled softly, but were quickly silenced by a snap from the white wolf.

"Brothers, I understand your anger, but there is good reason for caution. These monsters wield a mighty dark magic, strong enough to burn the fur from your hide and send you early to the wild hunt in the sky."

The white wolf nodded, "Yes manwolf, we will be cautious, but also cunning. These creatures will not be granted easy passage through our hunting grounds, but we will not be afraid, for the goddess smiles on us, and frowns upon them."

Jack was mesmerised by the bravery and passion in the white wolf's words, this feeling caused the row of sharp spikes rise the length of his spine.

Lupin and the white wolf talked and planned well into the night, while Jack curled up, wrapping his long tail around his body before finally falling asleep.

*

Jack awoke and stretched, not just warm in the midmorning sun, but really cosy. Then he realised that several small wolf pups, all snuggled into furry balls of warmth, surrounded him.

Then it hit him, his jaw dropped and he gave a small cry of amazement, he had transformed back into a boy! No green scales, no razor talons and with a small experimental cough, no fire!

He stood carefully as not to awaken the pups, shivering in the cool morning air, though the sun was beginning to warm his naked skin. The hilltop was empty save for the white wolf from the night before, standing sentry over the pack's pups.

A small campfire crackled and spat nearby with little black pot boiling away furiously, a small canteen of water and an old tin plate. Jack lifted the lid and sniffed, the wonderful aroma of beef stew made his stomach growl.

The white wolf nodded at a small worn leather pack, "Manwolf left this."

Jack had kept his telepathic abilities

He crouched and opened the pack, revealing an over-sized white shirt, an equally large pair of cloth breeks with a leather belt, but no boots. He quickly dressed, stuffing the shirt tails into his belt and tightening it to the limit. He was onto his second serving of the stew when Lupin galloped into the clearing.

Jack stood wiping his greasy chin on his sleeve, "Lupin! Look at me!"

"Indeed Jack, you have returned to your human form." He laughed at the boy's enthusiasm. He reached into his saddle bag and pulled out a pair of soft doeskin boots and tossed them to him. They were several sizes too large, but Jack packed them with soft grass and they fit well enough.

"I'm sorry Jack, I was so busy last night with my brothers that I forgot to explain your changeling ways properly. You see, each time you change," Lupin dismounted and placed a fatherly hand on his shoulder, "you will age faster."

Jack frowned, "Age? You mean...I will get older faster?"

Lupin nodded solemnly, "I am afraid it is the price we pay Jack." He stood and held open his hands, "I may look old to you, yet I am barely out of my teens. Being a Changeling is a gift Jack, yet it is a gift with teeth," he chuckled.

"But how did I change back?" asked Jack.

"Sleep Jack, we all change back in our sleep. Some of us have even learned enough magic to be able to change back at will. You may well learn it yourself in the future."

Jack was torn, fear and excitement filled his head. He certainly didn't feel any older, but if it was his destiny, then who was he to argue.

Lupin looked deep into Jack's eyes, "Jack, listen carefully."

Jack nodded, his excitement growing.

"There is something evil destroying these lands, and we need you to help us stop it."

Jack's pulse quickened, as he nodded again.

"In ancient times, demons roamed the earth, devouring and destroying. They were banished by the ancient wizard priests of Danu, using long lost methods and technologies. Now it would seem that something has crossed over, invited by a foolish young mage from Darkhaven. This abomination will seek ways to break the binding that hold his kind in their prison world, and unleash a new dark age of terror on the whole planet."

Images and fancies flew through Jack's mind. Huge heroes and mighty mages, terrible monsters and horrible battles. But how was he to help?

"We need you to travel far into the Northlands, even beyond the Giant's Teeth Mountains. Jack we need the help of the dragon clan to defeat these demons."

The Giant's Teeth? Dragon Clan? Jack thought they sounded fantastic, yet he had never travelled farther than the hilltop on which they now stood, and the thought of a distant adventure daunted him.

"You said I was watched all my life," said Jack, "Do you know of my family?"

Lupin saw the concern in the lad, but shook his head, "I am sorry Jack, Belthor is the man to question regarding your past. Put these questions and doubts from your mind and just change Jack, become a dragon again for the good of all. Seek the land of the dragons. Tell them all you have heard and then head for Ness. These wolves will hopefully help us find Lailoken and together we will try to stop the demon that possesses him."

Jack laughed nervously, "It seems I wont be a lad for much longer then eh?"

Lupin smiled sadly, pulling Jack into a tight hug, tears welling in his eyes, "So brave," he whispered , "and so young, for now…"

Chapter 4

Lailoken

The land was dying, sapped dry of the magic that was the source of its life. The trees had turned rotten and twisted, before finally giving up and falling across each other, as if they were trying to uproot and move from the corruption that tainted their forest. No bird sang, no animal burrowed and not even a single insect swarmed in the silence.

In the centre of the desolation stood a squat, windowless, square tower. Solidly built of large black stone blocks; a dark and foreboding building with a single heavy door. Waves of pure darkness seemed to radiate from between the bricks in pulses, rhythmic and powerful.

A distant high scream pierced the silence, sounding from deep within the bowels of the building, followed closely by a deep guttural laugh. It echoed from down a dark stairway of uneven steps, through a dank foetid corridor of roughly hewn stone, lit by oily smouldering torches, it ended in a room of horror.

The naked figure of an old man writhed upon a simple stone table, struggling in vain against invisible bonds that held him fast. His torso was daubed with glyphs and runes, which seemed to burn on the skin with a living flame.

"Speak the word mage," A too deep voice sounded from the inky shadows.

The captive resisted, arching his back till only his head and heels only touched the stone, small pools of sweat mingled with his blood beneath him.

The flames burned brighter, a soft sizzling followed and thin trails of smoke rose and the acrid aroma of charred flesh filled the chamber.

A long snorting inhale sounded, "You will never know how long I have lusted for this aroma."

A man dressed in a long black robe stepped from the shadow. Sweat ran down his shaven head, over his ashen face and dripped from his pointed chin. His thin lips were pulled back from his teeth in a rictus grin that did not suit his face and his eyes were sunken; ringed with deep shadows and as lifeless as a grave.

"Lailoken, please…," the captive begged through clenched teeth, "Fight it! Exorcise the demon…"

Somewhere, buried deep in the labyrinthine mind of the man in black, hid Lailoken. He was the foolish mage who had inadvertently opened the first portal to the Netherworld, allowing the demon that now possessed his body to gain control. Heedless of the warnings and even threats issued by the High Council of mages, Lailoken had secretly studied and practised the long-forbidden black arts. He had grown powerful and arrogant, shunning his family, teachers and friends alike before hiding himself in this vast forest, living wild and shielding himself with magical charms of reflection. There he constructed a simple, but strong tower, binding each stone with magical incantations that would render himself and his dark workings practically invisible to the probing spells of the High Council.

Now, in his own mind Lailoken whimpered pathetically, cringing at some of the terrible deeds he had committed over the fourteen years whilst under the control of the demon. He had desecrated the statue of his Goddess Danu in the Darkhaven Temple; he had ravished an innocent young priestess before slaughtering several acolytes. He had lusted for things beyond his understanding, and now he and all mankind were to pay for his ignorance.

Lailoken reached into the folds of his robe with a crooked hand and slowly produced several thin and wickedly sharp-looking spikes.

"Speak the word mage," he repeated softly; barely a hiss, right next to the captives ear, "and your end will be swift, if not..."

He clinked the spikes together, ominously.

The old mage took a deep shuddering breath, before attempting to compose himself in the face of almost certain death. He recognised the Necromius Spines from the texts he had studied as an apprentice. The dark iron was skilfully engraved with the runes and glyphs of the dark art of Necromancy.

He now knew in his heart that if he did not give up the word in this life, then this demon would doubtless tear it from his screaming soul in death.

"Yes!" Lailoken exulted, "each spine will be driven slowly into your energy centres, enslaving your soul, till I tired of my plaything."

"Danu forgive me!" he whispered, tears forming.

He took a slow deep breath; gathering strength and energy.

Lailoken stood stock-still, and if it was possible, his wide toothy grin grew in anticipation.

"**ATEH**," he screamed once.

The Word shook the room, sending a small shower of stones cascading from the ceiling, and deep in the hidden dimensions something fractured slightly; it was the ancient binding on the gateway to the Netherworld - The aeons old prison world created to hold the demons.

A small ball of purest darkness formed above the captive. Torches dimmed as it grew rapidly, till the mage could see his own ravaged frame, reflected in its oily surface. His eyes widened in terror as an inhuman face formed on the swirling gloss, all esurient eyes and terrible teeth.

The sphere settled next to the table and melted into a pool of pitch darkness, bubbling and hissing evilly.

Lailoken uttered a few harsh syllables, before swiftly grabbing the old mage and tossing him headlong into the rancid liquid. He barely had time to scream before being enveloped. Scant moments passed before a huge clawed fist thrust from the pitch fluid, followed closely by a pair of red eyes buried deep within a squat ugly face. The demon had large serrated tusk-like teeth jutting from an impossibly huge maw, and a long thin barbed tongue.

The shambling figure climbed out and stood on four powerfully muscled legs, swaying slightly before gripping the table with its taloned fist.

"Welcome to our world Krangresh!" Lailoken shouted with gleeful insanity.

The new demon turned and studied his liberator before speaking with a surprisingly clear voice, "Our time has come as you prophesied Master!"

Lailoken nodded, "Come brother, we have much work to do before we can free our brethren."

*

The huge iron-bound door swung slowly open, the rusted hinges squealing loudly in the silence. The newly reborn demon stepped outside, flinching in the brightness.

Lailoken laughed a harsh barking sound, "Feel it brother, that is sunlight! How long has it been? Ten millennia? Fifty?"

He placed a thin hand on the creature's flank and closed his eyes. The skin beneath his hand bubbled and smoked slightly as power flowed and the demon screeched and wailed, rearing and thrashing wildly.

A shadow crossed the sun as pendulous storm clouds brewed unnaturally. Lightning jabbed the clearing, exploding one tree in a flaming shower of splinters. The air crackled as living energy was sapped from the land and fed the transformation ritual. Powerful limbs shrank, eyes cleared and moments later a figure not unlike the old mage stood where the demon had been.

"I do not like this shape brother!" It spat scowling.

Lailoken laughed, handing his demonic brother the mages blue robe.

"Wear this and the cattle of this world will follow your words without question. Go brother, gather me a flock of priests, mages and shapeshifters; with their help we shall recite the six words of power that bind our kind. Then this shall be our world again, only this time forever..."

Chapter Five

The Giant's Teeth

Jack's shoulders burned, his tendons almost stretched to breaking. His stamina was wearing thin and exhaustion was beginning to take its toll. He was swept and buffeted on freezing winds, sometimes barely missing the cliffs and icy peaks of the Giant's Teeth, causing him to flap wildly to avoid a terrible crash.

Got to keep on going! He thought repeatedly, the small leather pouch gripped firmly in one fore paw.

I must not sleep. If I sleep then I will die.

He had been on the wing since the previous morning, almost two days now without rest or sleep; the urgency of his quest was spurring him beyond his normal endurance limits.

He climbed into the dark snow-laden clouds, then swooped down into the next glacier-cut valley, each peak harder than the last. It seemed that the Giant's teeth went on forever. Despair was growing with his weariness, fatigue and lethargy clouded his mind and with his one last sensible thought he sent out a shout; a cry for help.

"Dragons! Elders! Help me!" he began to weep, "Lupin! I cannot … do this…"

The water froze on his horned snout; the shining black ice of Dragon's tears.

Then through blurry eyes he saw the light, a bright shining flame in the snowy darkness. Then another, brief and bright, growing in luminosity. A chorus of deep booming voices surrounded him, spurring him on.

"Fly on brave brother!"

"Let our flame guide thee, brother!"

"Danu! Aid this young dragon, I pray thee!"

Three huge shapes swooped out of the darkness, bright flames spouting into the night.

"Set thee down young one, thou hast made it through the Teeth."

Jack's mind was muddled, he almost forgot he was in his dragon shape, yet the three guided him gently down.

Must be hallucinating, he thought sleepily, for the ground felt soft and warm.

Moments later he collapsed into a heap, barely able to lift his wingtips. Then he fell into the deepest sleep he had ever needed.

*

Jack awoke slowly and stretched sore muscles, blinking in the bright morning sunshine. He lay on a bed of soft green moss, and after his eyes adjusted to the sunlight, he was amazed when he realised that he sat in a clearing in a forest, ringed on the south side by towering mountains, capped with snow.

He was further astounded when he discovered the thick dark hairs that now coated his body and limbs, it appeared that he had aged several years over the last two days. Lupin's explanation of the Changeling ways echoed through his memory.

Jack stood and dressed. Lupin's clothes now fit perfectly. Instinctively he reached up and felt his face. A soft fuzzy beard grew on his cheeks and neck, and it itched furiously. His brown hair now hung in long locks halfway down to his waist. He tied it back from his face with a leather lace from his pack and hefted it onto his, now broad, back.

Suddenly his attention was snatched by a huge golden Dragon swooping, screeching from the clouds, directly at the clearing. Panic gripped him momentarily, but he decided to try and show no fear and stand his ground.

It swept down, mighty claws outstretched. Then at the last moment its huge leathery wings beat a mighty downdraft. The trees swayed in the roaring winds, losing some of their leaves. Jack staggered slightly but remained nearly motionless. The ground shook as the creature landed heavily, a long neck swung down and a mouthful of terrible razor teeth snapped the air barely an arms length away.

"Stay thy teeth!"

Another Dragon circled the clearing at the treetops, calling downwards.

The golden Dragon looked up then turned back and studied Jack, hot breath ruffled his clothes. It stank of sulphur and he was amazed how he never tasted it himself when he had used the shape.

The other Dragon landed, a brilliant green and yellow beast far larger than the first.

"What hast thou done with the Dragon left here last evensong?" demanded the green one in a stern, but level, tone.

"I will eat it!" Snapped the golden Dragon, baring his myriad teeth.

The green one growled, deep and low, the threat obvious. The golden one lowered his head in acquiescence, slowly backing off with his tail twitching.

"Answer!" The green one barked in his mind.

Jack was terrified of them, but tried not to show it. It took all of his courage and strength not to pee in his breeks.

"The Dragon was m…me," he stammered.

The green Dragon loosed an ear splitting roar that seemed to rumble and roll on and on, then the other joined him. It took Jack a while to realise that the creatures were laughing.

"I am a Changeling," he shouted over the raucous din.

Both ceased immediately and exchanged a curious look. Then without warning or word, they both disappeared over the treetops, flying swiftly northwards. Jack stood panting and trembling slightly, adrenaline coursing through his body.

"What in the name of the Goddess was that all that about?" He pondered aloud.

He wasn't about to sit around waiting for them to return. So he set off in the direction the pair had taken, moving swiftly between the ancient trees. A warm breeze sighed among the mighty boughs high above him as he ran on a bed of dry red needles.

The land began to rise and eventually the trees thinned and dwindled, the air cooled as the sun moved behind a mountain. Jack skidded to a stop, confused, as he realised that the sun was behind no mountain.

He stood gazing up at an enormous building, as tall and broad as a mountain its summit lost in the clouds. Several birds wheeled on high, soaring on the thermals. A frown slowly spread across his face as it dawned on him that they were not birds; they were Dragons.

He walked up to the base and examined the rock. Amazingly the surface of the stone was smooth and highly polished. Jack gasped as his reflection, tilting his head back slightly for a better look.

High above the Dragons seemed to take no notice of the tiny figure strolling around the base of their eyrie. Jack didn't want to change back into a dragon so soon, but he still had to find a way up to the summit. There he hoped he would find the help Lupin had asked him for.

He walked round the foot for an hour to no avail, the surface seemed flawless. He sighed and leaned forwards to rest for a moment, only the wall was insubstantial, and he fell painfully onto his hip. Jack cried out in surprise and blinked in astonishment; a narrow staircase was cut into the wall. It was invisible from the ground but when he trod upon the step it seemed to solidify beneath his feet. His head spun with a sickening dizziness, the illusion made him giddy.

"Magic!" he muttered to himself.

Jack raised a foot and tentatively moved it to where a step should be. Sure enough the step appeared and the one below vanished.

Right here goes he thought, moving slowly onwards and upwards. Before long he was high above the treetops, yet barely a fraction of the way up. If the climb took its toll on him physically, then the height or more likely the drop below took it's toll on him mentally.

A sheen of sweat covered his brow and the palms of his hands, yet still he climbed. His head spun with a sickening dizziness, the illusion made him queasy but on he trudged, on burning thighs. The sun crossed the sky in a wide arc as he passed from light to shadow, continually spiralling upwards.

A fine mist formed, blotting out the view below and above. He passed through the clouds, and up above them the sun burned bright in the wide azure sky. Farther up he now spotted platforms and caves built into the structure, the dragons now seemed far larger than he had first assumed. A dogged determination and raw rasping breath kept his legs and heart pumping hard.

"A Changeling art thou?" a familiar voice entered his mind. It was the golden Dragon, his long neck and head barred Jack's progress.

Before he could answer, the Dragon leapt from the ledge hooking Jack painfully with one huge taloned foot. He was lifted clear of the steps and swept high into the air. The wind tore the scream from his throat as they climbed higher, the eyrie below shrinking. Terror swept though him and above the Dragon laughed a deep and dreadful sound.

"A Dragon without wings? We shalt see…"

Jack did manage to scream as the talons holding his shoulders suddenly opened, and he began to fall.

Chapter 6

The Chosen

Jack cartwheeled into a tumble of sky and clouds, the wind robbing him of breath. Terror swept his memories clean as the shining stack of the eyrie rose from the blanket of white below. He twisted in the gale till his spinning ceased, the clouds far closer now. Desperation clawed at his mind as he sought to control his thoughts.

"Danu! Help me!" he cried a prayer.

A feeling of peace washed over him and as he pierced the damp clouds, the words of the change returned to him.

"Dragon Fly… Dragon Eye… Dragon Be…DRAGON ME!"

Bones broke and limbs lengthened as the change overtook him. Jack screamed silently in agony as he determinedly clung to consciousness. His clothing split and was ripped away in tatters by the howling wind. New muscles knit and grew, supporting his lengthening neck and spine.

He passed through the cloudbase in scant moments and was greeted by the green bowl of the valley floor rising swiftly. Jack's vision sharpened as the nubs on his back formed a pair of huge wings. He barely managed to snap them open, turning his fall into a swooping dive. The turbulence of his passing shook the trees as he shot across the valley at break-neck speed. Climbing into a swift right bank, he headed back towards the eyrie, momentum catapulting him through the clouds.

Fear turned to rage as his human emotions were fuelled by his Dragonish hormones. He inhaled deeply, loosing a shattering roar: A challenge to the golden beast high above.

Jack climbed swiftly through the sky building speed. His foe had settled on the plateau top of the eyrie and was peering over the edge into the clouds below.

Folding his mighty wings across his back and extending his talons, he dropped into a hawk-like dive.

The golden Dragon swung his head upwards too late as Jack slammed into him at full speed. The pair tumbled and crashed across the rocky rooftop, tails lashing, teeth gnashing and claws raking. The golden one roared in surprised fright and desperately fought back. The pair rolled back and forth, neither able to gain the upper hand.

Jack fought furiously but his opponent was fast and strong, and infinitely more experienced as a Dragon.

"CEASE!" Boomed a huge voice, "Stop thy combat now!"

Both rolled apart crouching low and panting heavily. The ground between them was littered with droplets of blood and several scales, predominately golden. In moments nine Dragons, of various sizes and colours, alighted around the pair.

The golden Dragon hissed and lowered his head to the dusty ground in deference as a huge red dragon stomped over to him, snapping his jaws loudly.

"Thou art too swift to fight." it chastened, "Yet again your impetuous nature hast done you wrong. For the Chosen one hast been wounded and his blood hast been spilt on this, the most sacred of places."

"This...thing, it...he is...the Chosen one?" the golden Dragon nodded at Jack, who now raised himself to full height, but remained silent, ready to spring into action if he needed to.

The red Dragon nodded slowly before fixing Jack with a piercing gaze. Jack matched the sparkling regard, his pulse quickening. A strange feeling filled him as the hypnotic stare began to make him sleepy. His breathing deepened and he struggled to keep his heavy eyelids open, unsuccessfully.

"Let slumber claim thee, Chosen..." the voice echoed around his foggy head, as he slowly curled into a deep sleep.

A radiant aura surrounded him as the Dragons moved into a wide circle around his prone body, snouts to the ground. An expectant hush fell on the gathering as the sun dipped behind the distant peaks of the Giant's Teeth. Then suddenly a blinding flash lit the top of the eyrie, causing several dragons to rear in fight, before fading to reveal the naked man still asleep. Several Dragons produced small spouts of flame, heating the air around him, warding off the chills of the night.

All night long the Dragon clan stood sentry over Jack's slumbering form, till the sun rose and morning stained the deep blue with a crimson wash.

Slowly Jack came to his senses, stretching and opening his eyes. Memories of the previous evening flooded back, and he leapt to his feet. The huge red beast still stood, towering over him, staring although now he looked down at the small hairy figure before him.

"Chosen, I bid thee greetings and a warm welcome to this, the Dragon's Enclave."

"Some welcome!" said Jack, then broke into a smile.

A rumbling roar swept around the plateau, as the gathered dragons began to laugh.

Jack leapt backwards as the golden Dragon approached, but he merely lowered his great head to the stone at Jack's feet and closed his eyes.

"I beg thy forgiveness." He said simply.

Jack looked up at the red Dragon, who returned his gaze intently.

"Well, I suppose so," he said somewhat reluctantly.

The golden Dragon whipped his head up and leapt nimbly onto his feet, loosing a roar and sending a jet of flame into the lightening skies, then sprang into the air and swooped from the eyrie, spiralling downwards.

Jack was puzzled. *Here's this Chosen thing again. Maybe Lupin's right.* He thought to himself. He was about to speak up when the red Dragon cut him off.

"I sense a query in thy head. Dost thou not understand thy responsibilities?"

"Responsibilities? I don't know what in the seven hells you are on about! *You* named me Chosen, after one of *your* kind attacked me! I sought you and the rest of the Dragons to beg for help, not..."

A furrow of a frown crossed the red Dragon's brow and he interrupted, stamping one huge clawed foot.

"Thou art the Chosen One! Many art the seasons we have waited for thou."

Jack nodded, acutely aware of the sheer size and strength of the red beast.

"We art the guardians of this granite tower, bound here by an ancient magic. We have to remain here till the Chosen One cometh and claims his rightful inheritance. He will enter the tower and secure our freedom forever!" It spoke with dangerous passion flashing in his dark red eyes.

Jack chose his words very carefully, "Red...May I call you Red? Enter the tower you say? Secure your freedom?"

The gathered dragons roared together, excitement sweeping the plateau.

Jack swayed unsteadily on his feet and his stomach growled painfully. He had not eaten for days and hunger was beginning to take its toll. Red sensed Jacks condition and barked a command. A green Dragon leapt from the summit, plunging into the clouds.

"I need your help Dragon," Jack addressed the leader

Red's brow furrowed again and his eyes narrowed to red slits as a deep rumble seemed to shake the ground, the tower itself seemed to vibrate alarmingly.

Jack staggered and the Dragons let out a low keening sound.

"MALKUTH..." A massive, deep voice sounded from the bowels of the earth, followed closely by a shattering sound.

The Dragons on the plateau went crazy, snapping the air in rage, roaring in frustration. Jack leapt clear as Red swept round in a circle gnashing his teeth. The gathered Dragons scattered, their roars deafening. Jack fell into a ball, holding his hands over his ears, quaking in terror.

Then as quickly as it came, the vibrations stopped. Instantly calm descended and the dragons landed, again noble and silent.

Jack unwrapped himself, and rose to his bloodied knees.

Red stood erect, snout held high sniffing, almost tasting, the air. He seemed to shake with barely concealed rage, and the heat that radiated from him made Jack take a step back.

"Again." he spat, "Another hath crossed."

More keening moans rang around the eyrie.

Jack stared in wordless amazement as a single huge tear ran down Red's snout and landed on the ground with a splash. A feeling of terrible sadness swept over him and he had to swallow hard, fighting the rising lump in his throat.

"The horde is pressing the master's binding. An evil beyond comprehension is sweeping forth to destroy all," Red spoke with soft sadness, "but despair not, for the Chosen shall triumph over the evil and we shalt once more be unbound."

Again the gathered dragons roared, this time with a fire in their hearts as well as their throats.

"What was that? That word...What was it? Malk..." Jack began asking terribly confused.

"NO" Red cut him off before he could finish the Word, "Thou must never utter the Word thou hast just now heard. It was used by the dark ones to break the second seal on the binding."

"Demons?"

Red nodded, "Tis been many an age since we have heard them called thus."

"That is why I came here," cried Jack.

Red nodded again, "That is the truth of it Chosen, thou must stop them."

It was Jacks turn to frown, then it dawned on him, it seemed that in helping the dragons, it would also help in the fight against the demons.

"Yes," Jack said rising to his feet, "I am your Chosen, just tell me where the entrance to this tower is."

"Behold" Red closed his eyes and a huge square glow formed on the ground, slowly it blurred and began to sink, each level revealing a deep step into the darkness.

Chapter 7

Approach and Receive

Jack stepped forward and nearly collapsed in a faint. Red swiftly caught him in one clawed fist and lowered him gently to the ground.

Seconds later the green Dragon returned with a freshly slain deer dangling from its firm grip. Red ripped the carcass into pieces and nudged the bloody mess at Jack.

"Eat Chosen, regain thy strength." He said.

Jack nearly vomited, the stench of the guts and entrails was overpowering.

"I need my pack, it fell…"

Unbidden, the golden Dragon swooped onto the plateau with the somewhat tattered bag in his claws. He landed lightly and offered the small pack to him. Jack took it with thanks and after dressing, quickly drank from his water bottle and used his knife to cut some chunks from the animals haunch.

"Err…" he began hesitantly, "You couldn't cook this could you? You know a small flame."

Red gave a sharp intake of breath. Jack cringed expecting the worst, but to his surprise the red Dragon blew a well controlled flame at the meat, chargrilling it in an instant.

Jack sat and devoured the food, crunching through the burnt skin, yet relishing every juicy mouthful. Soon his strength returned and the Dragons drew close as he made his way to the steps.

"Danu guide thy step, Chosen. May thy return be swift and sure." Red spoke for all the Dragons, who all lowered their heads in respect and anticipation.

Jack peered apprehensively into the oppressive gloom before taking the first of the deep, broad steps downwards. Strangely a flow of cool fresh air wafted from below on a slight breeze. Down he went, the square of light above disappearing as the passage took a spiralling descent. Light seemed to filter through the veins of quartz that ran through the granite, not bright, but enough to see the next step or two as he steadily progressed.

Wonder and confusion troubled Jack in equal measure as he stepped downwards. Mere days ago he had been a simple thief, a cut-purse and low born orphan. Now he was the Chosen, a Changeling sent on an unbelievable mission. Not only that, he was now a man, a stranger in his own body.

I wonder where Lupin and the wolves are by now, he thought. His thighs and calves began to burn and ache, unused to the seemingly endless steps in a never-ending corkscrew. His thoughts were like the stairway – spiralling - as he lost himself in thought.

Jack stopped dead in his tracks as the steps ended, opening out into an enormous octagonal room with a high vaulted ceiling, supported by sixteen huge pillars equally spaced around a circular dais. His heart raced as he stood in the entrance, for suspended in mid-air appeared to be a skeleton of some strange creature. A soft green glow radiated from the bones, reflecting in the glassy walls and casting deep shadows behind the pillars.

Jack stepped slowly into the room, passing one of the huge pillars. The skeleton, Jack realised, was not really human for the face was missing; it was a hollow dome of bone. The ribcage was solid, yet strangely segmented like an insects' chitinous shell, and covered with strange glowing, green runes, engraved deeply into the bone.

Suddenly it moved, the hollow head swivelled swiftly to face him.

Jack's own skeleton almost leapt through his skin as he stumbled backwards cracking his elbow painfully on the polished pillar. A faint hiss sounded over his panicked breathing, and slowly the head returned to face the way it had moments before.

Jack collapsed against the pillar, sliding down into a sitting position. He sat there till his heart settled and the cold sweat dried on his shaking hands.

"Huh! Some Chosen One I turned out to be."

Once again Jack approached the bones and this time simply stood and waited. Yet again the head turned to face him and suddenly a whisper sounded in his head.

"*Approach and receive...*" it said.

"Receive what?" Jack asked the faceless skull nervously.

"*Approach and receive...*" the whisper repeated.

Jack approached till he stood before the hovering bones, this time he was close enough to notice something glowing beneath the ribcage; it appeared to be the hilt of a dagger.

Jack felt compelled to reach for it, and as his fingers closed around the shining handle the skeleton moved again; but this time it leapt on him!

He fell back screaming, rolling from side to side desperate to dislodge the creature. It took him a few moments to realise that the bones were not attacking him, but were now encasing him. The ribcage was now a breastplate; solid yet flexible and the skull was now a helmet that fitted perfectly. His arms and legs were similarly enclosed, even his boots had a bone cover.

A feeling of dread swept though him as he wrestled to remove the helmet. It was stuck fast and Jack let out a low moan of despair.

"Please," he cried, tugging furiously, "Come off."

No sooner had the last syllable rolled from his tongue, the helm pulled easily free.

The whisper sounded again, "*You need only ask.*"

"Eh? Who said that?" Jack spun around.

"*I did, Ulfner Darkbane.*" The bones spoke softly in his head.

"Darkbane? The Banisher? Ulfner the Binder?" said Jack, his stomach churning.

"The same."

Jack nearly dropped the skull in shock. He now held the head of Ulfner Darkbane, the warrior priest who helped seal the gates of the Netherworld in ancient times.

"Replace the helm Jack."

Jack did as he was bidden, placing the helmet on his head. Then his eyes were drawn to the dagger lying on the floor, still shining. As he stooped to retrieve it Ulfner whispered again.

"Sword" Ulfner spoke.

Instantly the dagger transformed into a long sword and bright light danced in its intricate metalwork.

"Whip"

Again the weapon changed, this time a glowing whip tipped with flame. Jack held it tight, feeling strange energies flowing between it and the bones. All his aches and pains faded, the gnawing hunger receded and vigour flowed into every fibre of his being. Jack could feel Ulfner's feather light touch in his mind and it suddenly felt as if he shared his body. Dizziness made him reel for a moment but it passed swiftly as he became used to the feeling.

"Thank you Jack, you have arrived here in good time. The bounds are being unmade, the demons are once more rampaging." Ulfner's voice sounded louder and more like a real voice now, deep and full of power.

Jack nodded to nobody. "Yes, a mage called Lailoken has begun freeing the demons, Belthor and Lupin are trying to stop them." Jack paused, then added, he felt somewhat inadequately, "I have come here to try and get help from the Dragons..."

"VE GEBBURRAH..." another word of power rang out.

The room shook, massive fractures ran across the floor and great chunks of granite fell from the roof above.

The armour reacted faster than Jack ever could, making him dive and roll clear.

"Shield," Ulfer called using Jack's voice, and raising his arm above his head.

The whip instantly changed into a large oval shield, the rocks hit the surface and exploded into dust. Amazingly Jack felt no pressure as the blows rained.

A mighty cry rose from the deep darkness as something else crossed into the land of the living. Slowly the shaking receded and the choking dust settled.

Jack coughed up a lung-full of the fine powder, and rose shakily to his feet. Another demon had crossed, of that he was sure.

"There goes the POWER!" Ulfner cried angrily in Jack's mind.

Jack was confused, "Power?"

"First the Creator, then the Kingdom and now the Power. It is all part of the mighty binding."

Then Jack noticed a hole in the wall, through which a bright yellow light seemed to pour. He climbed the rubble and looked into a small cube-like chamber only slightly taller than he was.

There, in the middle floated a small sun!

"Come Jack," Ulfner spoke softly again, "Let us go and meet some friends of mine"

Jack climbed into the small room, and Ulfner made him place a bone gauntlet on the surface of the shining globe. The glow grew and enveloped Jack, then exploded noiselessly leaving only an empty space and dark shadows.

Chapter 8

Ulfenspan

Belthor had travelled eastwards, leaving Ness and the only hope for the future behind, he was sure the omens were right and that Jack would prove to be a worthy hero. Four days had passed since the lad had taken the flask, but so much had taken place. Three words of power had been uttered and the speakers killed or worse, and now Demons stalked the land. He had trekked almost constantly since leaving Ness, surviving on very little sleep, recharging his energy through meditation and prayer.

Now Belthor stood a solitary figure on the high ridge, the stiff breeze flapping his robe like a sail. He leaned wearily on his staff surveying the sweeping grasslands ahead. The morning sun reflected in the mighty river Ulfen, from those heights it appeared to be a shining snake slithering from the distant Giant's Teeth all the way to the sea far to the south. The huge river split the country in two, crossable only in one place; the amazing city of Ulfenspan.

For fourteen seasons Belthor had scoured the lands East and West of the Ulfen. He was sure beyond all doubt that Lailoken, was hidden in the West of the country, which meant that the demons would have to cross the river before passing on to the Capital. There the High Council of Magic convened. All the Gathering spells had been sent, and answered swiftly, so he hoped that they would act with haste.

Belthor muttered to himself angrily, "Debate, time wasting."

He had decided long ago that the Council was too encased in ritual and pompous ceremony, and that the land and people needed his ministrations more than they did.

He had warned them of Lailoken's interests, his secretive nature and his unsuitability for acceptance into the Mage University in Darkhaven. Yet they did not take his warnings seriously, till the braking of the first binding a few days before. Their heedlessness saddened Belthor, for he knew that many would pay for their ignorance, but the pain of their inaction was nothing compared to the hurt his soul suffered continually; for Lailoken was his own beloved son.

Belthor wiped a tear from his eye, and began pacing resolutely down the grassy slope, towards the river.

*

The sun was sinking into the late afternoon sky, as the vast towers of Ulfenspan rose into view. Seven huge buildings grew from the swift river, each housing a different noble family and their minions. The common folk were housed on the open road joining each tower, hundreds of houses lined the bridge-tops linking the towers. Belthor marvelled at the sheer size of the construction, as he did each time he crossed.

An enormous drawbridge was landed on the west bank. Chains, with each link bigger than a man, rose into the entrance and the huge portcullis hung open. Belthor was horrified to discover the West gate unguarded.

Surely they have been warned of the impending disaster he thought angrily.

He hurried inside, was immediately stopped in his tracks. His innate sixth sense told him danger was near. The wide stone steps rose into the building, and stopped at a huge pair of closed iron-bound wooden doors. He climbed the steps slowly, offering a prayer of protection to Danu. The faint click of his staff on the worn stone was the only sound he could hear, that and his own laboured breathing. Ulfenspan usually rang with a vivacious hubbub, and as Belthor stopped at the doors the silence disturbed him immensely.

He placed a hand on the door and immediately withdrew it as if it were hot. Peering closely he could see the deep polished varnish was blistering and peeling in a hand print.

A Demon has touched that very spot mere hours ago, he surmised.

Belthor drew a deep breath, his face contorting in terrible fury; the demons were an insult to life, an abomination, and a corrupt taint that harmed his Goddess and her children. Summoning the deep power that ran through him like the river below, he swung the metal tipped staff at the door. A flash of brilliance and a surge of power, then the doors exploded into splinters.

The scene that greeted him turned his stomach. A single body lay behind the door studded with a dozen or more arrows. That was the easy bit, around the entrance hall dozens of soldiers lay dead, hacked and chopped, stabbed and sliced till the last man fell.

Belthor moaned for the souls of the fallen soldiers. In his mind's eye he could read the situation. The Demon would have walked in, deliberately letting the body be destroyed. Then it would wreak its terrible havoc; possessing the first soldier, who would kill his friends before being killed himself. Then on to the next poor soul, tirelessly killing everything in its path. The carnage and coppery smell of death was overpowering.

A swift whispered incantation and the bodies flared into flames, burning to ash in moments. Things were worse than his most terrible nightmare could conjure. Belthor broke into a run, his knee joints protesting.

The beast must be on the bridge top by now, he thought, his mind racing.

Along the corridors and up the stairs he flew. Bodies lay here and there; servants mostly. At the head of the last stair lay the body of an old man, crumpled in the corner. A red flower of blood blossomed on his chest, as the Lord of the tower he must have been the last man alive to face the creature before it attacked the population outside.

Belthor burst out into the evening air, gulping the sweet freshness. Amazingly the streets were empty, he prayed that the population had evacuated the bridge and made for the relative safety of the next tower, or beyond. He waited moments, trying to sense the Demon, unsuccessfully.

The narrow streets were packed with houses, mostly wooden, but well built and solid designed to survive the high winds that ravaged the plains each season. As he moved quickly past the apex of the bridge, Belthor spotted a furtive movement in one of the small windows of the Keystone Inn. He stopped and pointed his staff at the building.

"Face me demon, in the name of the Goddess," He cried.

Nothing moved, then a small bird landed on the sign above the door. It began to sing its night song before taking to the wing again.

Belthor relaxed nothing as fragile as a tiny bird could abide the aura of a demon. He strode confidently to the door and rapped with his staff.

"Open up," he called to the occupant, "The Demon is gone, please let me in."

Again nobody answered.

"Open," he rapped with a magic knock.

The stout door swung inwards with a clatter. Belthor did not flinch as the crossbow quarrel flew past his cheek, the feather buzzing his ear.

"The next one will go through your eye demon." Cried a frantic female voice.

"Be calm my child," soothed Belthor unfazed.

He projected peace and light into the room; spreading a sense of wellbeing and love, standing with open arms he waited showing no threat.

A bedraggled young woman stepped from the gloomy shadows, her fine green dress was blood spattered and torn, long blond hair hung in filthy rat's tails, and a gleam of madness shone in her beautiful almond shaped brown eyes. She stood wavering, yet held her crossbow with a vice-like grip.

"Is…is it…over?" she almost begged, huge tears spilling down her dirty face.

Belthor smiled sadly, placing a hand on her troubled brow.

"Sleep child, forget the horror. Remember the good times and the pain will pass."

The woman sighed and collapsed into the crook of his strong arm, fast asleep. As Belthor carried the girl to the gate of the next tower he healed her fragile mind.

"Halt" cried a voice high on the parapets.

Belthor set the girl gently on the ground and looked up.

"He has killed Samanthiel. Call the Lord."

"The girl is unharmed, she is well physically but carries scars that she will find harder to bare." Belthor added, "She sleeps."

"Who goes there?"

Belthor grew tired of the nonsense and tapped the ground with his staff.

"Open now," his voice was amplified by the magic and the great door swung silently open.

A man in black leather armour met him at the door. Tall and imposing, he carried himself with an unmistakable air of authority, though he carried no weapon. His handsome chiselled features were criss-crossed with fine scars, and his long black hair was tied severely into a topknot. A tight unit of guards, similarly armoured, followed closely behind him. Belthor was glad to see that none was armed.

Perhaps they have learned from their brothers mistakes, he thought.

"It worked then..." the man said simply, relief written all over his pale face.

"What...did...you...do?" Belthor demanded, suspicion writhing like a coiled snake squirming in his guts.

"It wanted our healer..." the man blinked, "and we gave her."

.

Chapter 9

A Demon Approaches

Krangresh the Demon was furious, insane rage drove him onwards, despite the damage his body had taken. He clenched his fists and screamed in frustration, the unearthly sound shattering the silence of the forest.

Yet again the shadows erupted with growls and howls, fangs bit and sliced swiftly, before the enemy melted back into the night.

With a few uttered guttural syllables and an outstretched palm, a nearby tree exploded into flames. The light swept away the shadows, revealing dozens of wolves; eyes bright with reflected fire; hackles risen and ears folded flat; muzzles bloodied with shining fangs bared.

The nearest wolf leapt as the rest scattered into the night. Two large paws hit the Demon's chest, causing him to stagger and trip over a fallen branch. The brave wolf began tearing at the face and neck of the fallen creature, before a single powerful hand closed around its furry throat. A terrible yelp of fear and pain sounded as black flames swept from the fist. The shaggy fur around its throat burned as the grip tightened. Desperately the wolf fought to escape, howling piteously. Moments later the charred, lifeless animal was tossed into the bushes.

Krangresh roared triumphantly through tattered lips, before resuming his relentless march. The wolf clan had hindered the demon for hours, but at a terrible cost; eight brave wolves had lost their lives so far. The wounded Demon now limped Southwest, stopping neither for food or rest.

*

Lupin rode hard; crouching low in the saddle, trusting his horses night-vision as they flew between the trees, before the forest thinned, then opened out onto sweeping grassland. Starlight lit the sleeping land, and showed the small city of Ness in the distance.

He felt terrible leaving his brethren, but he needed to get ahead and warn the city. He hoped that the High Council had acted on Belthor's warnings, they might even have developed some sort of defence strategy.

The sun rose and a deep uneasiness settled on his shoulders as he crossed the cultivated farmlands; no ditches surrounded the crumbling walls, no pit-traps, nothing. There didn't even appear to be soldiers on the gates.

Sparks flew from his horses iron shoes as he clattered through the cobbled streets, startling the early risers. The city council square was almost deserted, apart from a couple of bored looking guards.

Lupin leapt from the saddle and grabbed a small guard roughly, almost lifting him clear of the cobbles.

"Summon the Captain of the Guard," He almost roared, "The Lord, everyone."

The small guardsman struggled, then drew a small silver whistle, which he blew till his face turned purple.

Lupin lowered the man, before he was cudgelled into unconsciousness and the darkness claimed him.

*

Lupin came-to in the market square, his head and hands held securely in the tight wood of the stocks. Judging the height of the sun, he realized that he had been unconscious for an hour or more. Curious city folk surrounded the platform along with a ring of guards.

"Please free me," he cried, straining to catch a guard's eye, "There is a demon coming, it will kill you all…"

The Captain turned to face him, a solid looking man in his fifties. His hair cropped so short, almost shaven and dressed in a battered breastplate and hard leather armour. He carried himself with the confident ease of a seasoned fighter..

"A Demon eh?" his gravelly voice interrupted his ranting.

Lupin twisted in the stocks, giving the man a hard stare.

"Yes Captain, a demon. By tomorrow morning your city will be in chaos, many people are going to die."

The Captain held his gaze for several seconds, before flinching.

"Free him," he barked to his men, "Return his weapons and possessions. Now."

Lupin stood, rubbing the lump on the back of his head.

"Thank you Captain." He said.

He nodded, "Tell me." Was all he said.

Lupin was glad the Captain seemed sensible, so he quickly related the whole situation to him, holding nothing back. As he finished the Captain drew a small hip flask, and downed a generous swig of alcohol, then offered it to Lupin, who declined.

He smiled grimly, "We better get his Lordship out of his pit then eh?"

The pair strode swiftly through the crowd towards the castle. The word "Demon" could be heard echoing around the crowd in fearful whispers.

"Have the Magic Council sent anyone here yet?" Lupin enquired.

The Captain snorted, the only answer he needed to give.

"Then I think we had better think about evacuation."

The Captain stopped.

"D'you have any idea of the number of civilians in this city? Thirty-five thousand and that doesn't include the illegals from Grimswade and Haarsfalt. Prob'ly nearer forty."

Lupin sighed, "Captain, this one solitary demon will scour this city, killing randomly and influencing anyone with evil in their hearts to do the same. It will not leave till it finds a magic user."

"Magic users?"

"Mages, Priests, Druids, Healers, Witches or Changelings."

They marched along an increasingly busy main street.

"Don't think we got many of those sorts here. Well…we have got a couple of temples"

"You would be surprised, Captain."

The castle suddenly loomed, tall for the city; four stories. Four small towers rose from the corners another level, and all surrounded by a low crenelated wall.

Lupin was surprised to find Lord Ness descending the steep stairs from the main gate to meet them. He was a tall slender man with a long face, framed by long silver hair, hanging in thick braids, dressed in a long red overcoat and a purple cape embroidered with the city crest; crossed swords behind a shield embossed with a boat and a sheaf of wheat. A golden hilt shone at his hip, but Lupin guessed it was more ceremonial than practical.

He stopped before Lupin a thin hand extended.

The Captain lowered his head in a show of respect.

"No need for formalities Reed," he spoke in a deep sad voice.

Lupin shook the hand, surprised at the firm grip.

"Lupin," he said simply.

"Yes, I know of you Lupin. My eyes and ears tell me many disturbing things. Things that should only be whispered over jugs of ale in smoky taverns."

"Demons"

Ness nodded slowly, a distant look in his eyes.

"I am familiar with the prophecies, Lupin. Belthor is a dear friend, we have spent many evenings in the same tavern, whispering…"

Relief flooded through him, no persuasion was needed.

"Lupin, you seem to think that the demon is seeking magic users. Well…" he paused taking a deep breath, "If we remove the magic, then surely the demon will go elsewhere, even follow them…into a trap perhaps?"

Lord Ness's reasoning was sound, it had the kernel of an idea, but how would they trap and hold a powerful demon against its will, Lupin mulled over the idea.

"Reed, gather my housemen. Co-ordinate with the guard, I want every Cleric, Priest, Witch and Warlock here by noon."

Captain Reed snapped a crisp salute and disappeared inside the castle.

"Come Lupin, we have plans to draw up."

Chapter 10

Necromius Spines

Jack stood with his bone gauntlet resting on the glowing globe. He barely managed to avert his gaze before the glow had swallowed him. He staggered slightly as a dizzy spell swept over him, and even though his eyes were screwed tight shut, the light still hurt. It seemed to make him light as a feather and his grip on the orb tightened as his bone boots lifted from the floor. The light began to pulse rapidly and the armour enveloping him slid off a piece at a time. The pulsing slowed and Jack lowered gently, till his feet touched the floor. The brightness dimmed to a soft glow and he tentatively opened his eyes. It took him a few moments to realise that the presence of Ulfner seemed to have left him.

Jack saw that he was still in the same chamber, though the roof was now intact. He stepped into the octagonal room, halting before a basic stone table in the centre of the dais. Ulfner's bones rested upon the smooth surface, still glowing a faint green.

A low hum vibrated the room and the luminous runes flared brightly and then vanished before a nimbus of green particles formed around the bones. He rubbed his eyes and took a back step as the bones began to knit together; the face formed, the segmented ribcage broke noisily into individual ribs and all the small bones magically shaped themselves from the green motes. He watched aghast as pulsating organs swelled, appearing in the hollows of the now complete skeleton. Sinews, muscle and skin snaked and slithered forming the complete body. As Jack stepped closer, thick dark hairs began sprouting across Ulfner's massive barrel chest and abdomen.

Ulfner Darkbane was a giant of a man built like a bull with broad shoulders and thick neck, but with the slim physique of an athlete.

A row of thin black spikes were puncturing his skin; one in his forehead; one between his bushy brows; one in his throat; one in his heart; one in his solar plexus; one in his belly button and a final one in his groin. Each spike was engraved with tiny runes that glowed with the same green that had previously covered the bone armour. Jack leaned over the huge frame and studied the spikes closely and was amazed to find that the inscriptions seemed to be moving slowly, creeping and crawling in spirals down into Ulfner's body.

Jack gingerly touched the forehead spike with the tip of one finger.

"COME ON LAD! PULL THE NECROMIUS SPINES FROM ME" Ulfner's voice boomed into his mind, making him leap back in fright.

He gripped the spine and heard echoes of great magical words ringing through the metal, **"Ateh... Malkuth... Ve Gebburah... Ve Geddulah... La Ohlam... Amen."**

As the last spine was removed from the body, the wounds sealed themselves over, vanishing completely after a moment. Ulfner took a deep whooshing intake of air, then suddenly sat up. He reached out with two hands the size of shovels and gasped Jack's head cupping his palms around his ears.

Through the muffling hands Jack heard a quiet mumbling sound, this grew to a loud high pitched whistle and ended in a terrible scream. The sound was actually painful, causing his teeth to chatter and a thin line of blood to run from his nose the coppery taste unsettling him. A tingle ran from the base of his skull, down his spine and right to the tips of his bare toes.

Ulfner lifted his hands away, and Jack wiped at the blood trickling down his bare lip. He was further astonished to discover that the hair that had previously covered him was gone, he also felt different.

Then it hit him, he was young again.

Ulfner stood and gave a luxurious stretch, making his bones pop and crackle grinding noisily.

"Do you know just how good that feels?" he said.

Jack shook his head, in awe of the big man standing before him.

"I have been pinned there for many years…far too many."

Jack looked up at the man towering over him with his huge lantern jaw and full jutting lips, topped by a hooked nose with flaring nostrils. But it was Ulfner's eyes that really held his attention more than his sheer bulk, for one eye was piercing green and the other was a deep crimson.

"Those words…" Jack began.

"The Mighty Binding," Ulfner interrupted answering his question before he asked it.

"What do they mean?" asked Jack.

Ulfner smiled, "Well to put it simply, young champion, it means: By the Will of the Creator; Her Kingdom; Her Power; Her Glory; Forever and for all Eternity; So Be It."

Jack frowned thinking he had heard some old temple preacher shouting something similar, what seemed like an age ago.

Ulfner nodded, "Yes similar Jack, merely the words but without the real power of the creator behind it."

Ulfner reminded Jack of the old mage Belthor, answering the unspoken questions as he did.

"Why were you pinned there Ulfner?"

"We foresaw the inevitable release of the demons, Jack and I was pinned here so my bones could act as a portal linked to the future, to the time when you would find them. My Angels were also pinned into forms of their own - albeit slightly lesser prisons than my own here."

"Angels?" Jack was puzzled.

Ulfner nodded, then stepped across to a large stone container beside the entrance to the stairs. He lifted the thick stone lid, making the thick cords of muscle on his arms bulge. Holding it open with one hand he reached in and produced a shimmering robe of green silk, which he slipped on.

"Come Jack, let's go and see how the struggle is going."

Ulfner made towards the door. Suddenly he realised that he did not have the weapon he had wielded before being transported here. He was about to call after Ulfner when he found the shining dagger had magically appeared in his right hand. It seemed he need only think of it and the weapon would appear.

Jack scrambled after Ulfner as his broad back disappeared around the central column of the spiral staircase. As the pair walked Jack quizzed the mage.

"Angels you said, actual Angels? With wings and all?"

Ulfner laughed to himself, a deep friendly rumble, "The Angels you are thinking of are the archetypal beings mentioned throughout history in texts and holy documents. The *real* Angels, *my* Angels…are slightly…different."

Chapter 11

Betrayal

Belthor stood still, the simple statement had paralysed him with shock.

"You...gave...her?" He repeated slowly. The man nodded.

Without warning Belthor swept his iron tipped staff up in a swift arc and it connected with a satisfying thud, knocking the stunned man back onto the stairs. The gathered guards gave a shout and made to seize him, but Belthor raised his hand and uttered one powerful word.

"Stop"

The men became rooted to the spot, able to move and breath normally but transfixed nonetheless. Belthor stooped and picked up the sleeping girl as their leader spat a bloody tooth upon the broad stone step, his handsome face now marred by a swollen purple mark on his jutting jaw. He sat up and touched his cheek gingerly, wincing slightly at the throb.

"Take me to the Seeing tower immediately." Belthor ordered, and added, "...and take this girl to more comfortable surroundings, she will sleep for several hours." He passed her to one of the bigger guards.

"Who do you think you are, coming here and assaulting a Tower Lord?" The man demanded angrily.

Belthor stiffened and took a deep breath, then he closed his eyes for a moment; gathering energy. When he opened them it appeared that his pupils had been replaced with molten gold, a fierce light burned shining with power.

"A Tower Lord would not sacrifice a simple healer to save his own pathetic life. So I will ask this once: Take me to the seeing tower immediately, before you incur my wrath and regret your inaction."

The Lord quailed, paling visibly; his arrogance evaporating like a small puddle on a summer's day.

"Cease." Belthor said, giving a small nod.

The men on the steps stumbled and fell to their knees as the magic released its grip on their feet.

Their toothless Lord stood shakily and called a man, "Do as he bids, take him to the mage's room at the top of the third tower."

*

The guard led Belthor through the city to third tower in the middle of the river and upwards into a narrow staircase. This led to a poorly lit, cramped passage, criss-crossed with spider webs, rarely used by anything other than insects. Both men had to stoop slightly to avoid banging their heads on the low beams.

Before long a shining black door offered a reflection of the guard's burning torch and he stood aside to let Belthor approach the seemingly impenetrable barrier. The old mage reached out and placed one hand on the shining surface, straightening his crooked fingers.

"Open." Belthor whispered.

A pulse of light spread through the dark door followed by a hiss. The guard retreated two or three steps as the barrier glowed in the frame, then exploded in a shower of sparks, leaving him blinded momentarily.

"Please summon the remaining Tower Lords." said Belthor, "Have them meet me here as soon as possible."

"Yes Sir." He said nodding, before scurrying off into the gloom.

*

A simple stone bowl and jug stood upon a plain wooden table standing in the middle of a square room. The room itself was equally plain with no further furnishings and only bare stone for walls and flooring.

Belthor filled the bowl with water till it almost overflowed, he stood with his back to the doorway and placed his hands on the tabletop. He peered into the dark depths of the reflection, looking beyond the bowl and far further afield. He slowed his breathing; relaxing deeply before sending out his awareness, seeking the mind of Riznar - the leader of the Council of Mages in Darkhaven.

After a moment the water shimmered and a man's pale face floated into view. It was sagging and thin with dark circles surrounding pale, ice-blue eyes, a bulbous nose topped thin lips drawn into a tight line. Recognition lit the eyes and a scowl darkened the face.

"Ah Belthor the wanderer returns in our greatest time of peril…" The high nasal tones echoed in Belthor's head.

"We have no time for this Riznar. Why have you not sent the battle mages? Where are the defences?" Belthor interrupted getting straight to the point.

A small smile flickered across Riznar's face, "Belthor, we trust you have discovered the whereabouts of your wayward offspring, after all it has been fourteen seasons has it not?"

A pang of pain stabbed into Belthor's heart, and a frown crept across his face. Riznar smiled openly at Belthor's discomfort.

Belthor sighed and closed his eyes for a moment, "I hope the Goddess Danu forgives your dark soul as easily as I do Riznar, for I fear you will be pacing the seven hells for eternity if you do not mend your ways."

Beaten, Riznar gave up the sparring.

"The Demon plague has been prophesied for centuries Belthor. Nothing we do will prevent this from happening, not even this mad Changeling prophecy you pursue so tenaciously." He paused drawing an expansive breath, "…So we have decided to give up the Western province allowing the city of Ness to fall to them. We need you Belthor to cross the Ulfen and collapse the city into the waters. They must not have a useable passage across the river."

"What!" Bethor thundered, "Are you willing to abandon thousands of people and animals to the demons?"

Riznar's face was impassive, "We have to protect the capital, Belthor. The University of Magic…"

"You want to save yourself Riznar. You and your council of cronies, sit in your high towers, distant from nature and man. Do you really think the demons will not be able to build boats or journey into the Giant's teeth and cross at the source?"

"We have plans to build a magical defensive wall on the East bank of the river. Any beast crossing the water will be dealt with and swept out to sea." Riznar spluttered, his voice rising I pitch; sweat forming on his brow and lips.

"From your high wall you may well just be able to see the people lining the far bank before the demons claim them…Lick your lips and swallow Riznar, that is the sour taste of death." Belthor gripped the edge of the table so hard that the wood cracked.

Before Riznar could respond Belthor gave an angry cry and smashed the bowl, sending water and broken pottery flying in all directions. He turned and discovered an audience of six regal men, the one with the swollen jaw he recognised, the rest merely stood silently, half hidden in the gloom.

"My Lords," Belthor began wearily, "It seems we have a big problem facing us."

Chapter 12

To Trap a Demon

The afternoon sun was warm as Lupin stood before the walls of the city, coils of silver chains in his hands and a small branch of a rowan tree stuck in the earth at his feet. Even though the chains were blessed and anointed by several priests, for the first time in his life he felt real fear gnawing like some parasite in his guts. They felt strange in his hands, warm and cold at the same time, almost as if they buzzed with a life of their own.

The field ahead was empty, newly tilled by a farmer and to Lupin the rich dark soil smelt alive. Several more rowan branches dotted the land in a wide circle around him, these had been carefully placed by the coven of witches less than an hour earlier, and he had been given strict instructions by them not to remove even one twig from the leafy limbs.

The ground thrummed and vibrated all around him, a heat haze rose shimmering the horizon as he waited. Then the wolves appeared from the distant grasslands, dozens of them bounding across the field towards him

From the crumbling walls above Lupin heard a man cry out, "Captain, wolves! Shall I deploy the archers?"

Lupin turned and growled, a dangerous light flashing in his dark eyes, "Do not fire on these animals! They are my kin."

The walls were lined with archers and priests, led by Lord Ness himself. Their arrows had been dipped into the holy fountain in the temple and the witches had performed a complex ritual over them; calling down the powerful blessings of the moon and sun. The sharp metal tips were now luminous and sparkling in the sunlight.

The wolves raced into the circle unharmed and yapped and yelped excitedly. Lupin knelt and touched heads with the white wolf as the pack surrounded them.

"You have done well brothers, the Demon will head right here into our trap, you have my thanks and the thanks of these humans. They have decreed it illegal to hunt wolves from this day forth. I have to bind this beast and hopefully any more that follow."

"We will stand with you Manwolf." The white one said.

Lupin shook his head sadly, "No Brother, your fight is over. Go now lose yourself in the deep forests to the Southwest, live in peace and may our bright sister moon smile upon you always."

White growled but lowered his head in submission, and with a short bark the pack veered off to the Southwest and relative safety.

*

Moments later a second cry went up from the walls above, but Lupin's sharp eyes had already picked up the shambling figure approaching. A piercing cry, thin and hungry, rang across the land as the Demon spotted his prey waiting. The stumbling became a half run and cries of horror rose from behind Lupin as the watchers above saw the creature in greater detail.

One thin arm was hanging off at the elbow, while the other had grown grotesquely huge with a sharp claw where the hand had been. It no longer resembled a man, the face torn and raw with one eye missing and it dragged an injured leg behind; using the remaining leg and the misshapen arm to move.

Lupin's breath came in short pants as the chains in his hands wriggled and writhed violently like shining metal snakes. He tensed, wrapping the chains around his knuckle on his right hand and hanging in a loose loop on the left.

The Demon stopped suddenly at the outer limit of the rowan branches. The two nearest branches glowed a soft green, then a bright white barrier formed between them. It took a stumbling step towards the light and the hiss of charred flesh filled the air.

"Archers! Legs only. Legs only! Loose!" Lord Ness roared.

Twenty glowing arrows flashed though the air, half hitting their mark. The demon's one good leg resembled a pincushion before it stumbled and fell face first into the earth. Lupin leapt into action, bounding across the field and pulling the rowan branches as he ran. The Demon tried to stand but collapsed again, as Lupin planted the branches in a new circle around the stricken beast, then leapt upon its back and looped the chain around its neck and torso. The chains tightened and glowed a fierce white then tightened again. The demon screeched in rage, pain and maybe even fear.

Lupin tried to leap clear as it tried to reared up one last time, amazingly the long arm snaked out and the hooked claw slashed a terrible cut across his back and shoulder. Lupin gave a gurgling cry and fell between the rowan branches. The Demon sensed the injured Changeling within its reach and slowly began to pull itself forward with the terrible hook.

Lord Ness and several priests sprinted to the fallen Lupin. They pulled his arms as the hook thudded down on his foot slicing off the toe of his boot along with a couple of toes. The rowan barrier sprang to life glowing brighter than before and the demon quickly retracted the arm. It lay there bound by magic but still deadly, its influence played on the minds of the priests but they wore amulets and wards protecting them from the worst of the taint. It slowly licked the bright blood from the hook and gurgled a horrible laugh.

"My brothers will free me soon enough..."

"Post a mage on the wall, let nobody approach this monster upon pain of death." Lord Ness commanded, as the priests took Lupin to the keep to tend to his wounds.

Lord Ness could feel the dark mind-tendrils of the beast probing the shield around his own mind, as it lay there waiting with infinite patience. As he walked away from the field he felt a sudden heart wrenching sadness and a distant, terrible pain.

"VE GEDDULAH." The word of power rang out.

A tremor ran through the land and thunder rumbled off to the Northwest, and in the gutter the demon began to laugh with a hellish glee; an insane giggling that tore at Lord Ness's senses.

"The Glory..." He whispered leaving the Demon alone for now.

Chapter 13

Wild Angels

Jack and Ulfner emerged into a world of dark twilight; no stars lit the sky, just an oppressive black blanket of nothing.

"Welcome to the Netherworld Jack." said Ulfner.

"The Netherworld? Isn't this where the demons are imprisoned?" Jack asked warily casting a glance over his shoulder.

Then it dawned on him that they stood upon a flat featureless plain, not the tower of rock he expected.

Suddenly a deep boom shook the air making Jack leap in fright.

"That's them. The Demon horde are continually testing the Binding, seeking a way back to the world of the living. They are so close that they can almost taste it." Ulfner explained.

Another boom sounded, followed closely by a distant flash of light. It lit up a small square building in the distance before the darkness swallowed it again.

Ulfner reached into the folds of his robe and produced a small silver orb, which he proceeded to toss into the air. The ball hung in mid air above his head then burst into light. Jack squinted in the brightness and stumbled backwards quickly as the shadows receded to reveal dozens of black demons; a misshapen, writhing rabble of vicious faces full of teeth and eyes, with twisted limbs that invariably ended in a claw or hook.

Jack leapt closer to Ulfner and twisted quickly, realising that they were completely surrounded. The Demons were edging slowly forwards into the bright pool of radiance, Ulfner seemed to chuckle gleefully to himself and he turned to Jack with a strange look in his colourful eyes.

"Now might be a good time to draw upon the weapon Jack."

"Sword." said Jack quickly.

The weapon sprang into his hand from nowhere, but it now burned with a bright flame of the purest white. Jack's sword arm twitched and trembled, the sword buzzing almost alive in his grip. A bizarre feeling of joy coursed through his body; it seemed that the sword was delighted to be drawn

"Staff," Ulfner boomed. A long weapon appeared in his meaty fists, tipped on each end with a ball of green flames.

Suddenly with a screeching war cry, Ulfner plunged into the mass of demons, his staff a whirling green circle of destruction. More screeches sounded but these were the pained cries of the injured monsters.

Without thinking Jack leapt after him, his sword whistled a keening cry of its own. Time slowed as Jack performed a dance of death among the creatures; hacking and slashing, chopping and cleaving. He was amazed to find that the demons actually melted before him, shrinking back from the bite of the bright blade. A fierce joy coursed though his veins and he seemed to slip into a trance, fighting automatically, not really aware of the hideous din or the terrible stench of the Demons. Jack was sliced with various superficial wounds, it was not till one beast he had cut down managed to sink its fangs into his calf, that he actually felt any pain.

Then he fell.

"Shield." He managed before a small Demon leapt with four arms raking the armoured surface in a fearsome frenzy.

"Spear." Jack cried thrusting the point into the gaping maw of the Demon.

Ulfner raised a silver horn to his lips and blew a single clear note, which was answered instantly by a chorus of notes ringing in from various directions. The battle stalled as ten huge glowing figures appeared in a circle around the Demons.

A huge cry of despair rang out from the Demons, and they made an attempt to flee, but most were slain by glowing arrows or fiery sword thrusts.

Jack pushed the fallen Demon from his chest and feebly tried to stand as a gigantic bearded man in a silver breast plate, strode over the fallen Demons and raised his flaming sword to strike him.

"Zadkiel, stay your hand." Ulfner barked.

The giant turned his fierce face towards Ulfner then frowned. He leaned close and sniffed at Jack, before lifting him easily with one hand.

"This is no Demon," a mellow voice boomed in surprise.

Jack felt safe in the grip of the giant named Zadkiel, he guessed that he had to be at least three times the size of a full grown man with grotesquely muscled arms and legs, even Ulfner appeared small beside these giants.

Jack slipped into unconsciousness as the group headed towards the building.

*

When he awoke his leg no longer hurt, the leather of his leggings were torn and bloodied but the flesh appeared intact. He looked around and saw that he lay on a bed in a square windowless room with one single large wooden door. Ulfner sat on a chair in the corner of the room, murmuring with his eyes closed.

"Your wounds do not last here Jack. That is the nature of this hellish place; you cannot leave it through death, though the pain is real. Actually it was quite refreshing after all the years of boredom." He said.

Ulfner opened his eyes, "Come Jack, I will introduce you to the Angels."

Jack climbed down from the bed and tested his leg, sure enough it was as good as new. He followed Ulfner through the door and into a large hall. The floor was polished granite and the walls hung with tapestries showing life; Animals, birds, fish, trees, mountains and rivers; all beautifully embroidered with lifelike imagery. At a huge round table sat the ten silent Angels, still as statues.

Ulfner pushed Jack forwards, and began his announcement

."Brothers, this is the Chosen One. He will lead you to freedom and reunite us with the Goddess."

At that the gathered Angels all turned and fixed him with an intent gaze, Jack squirmed under their close scrutiny.

"Jack, allow me to introduce our Angelic brethren; first you have already met Zadkiel with his over zealous sword arm."

The gathered Angels chuckled and Zadkiel nodded to Jack; in the light of the room he did not look so hideous as he had in battle. He had a round face with the bushiest beard Jack had ever seen, framed by a wild mane of dark hair cascading down over his round shoulders. He had a sharp pointed nose that poked out of the beard, topped by black eyes that did not appear to have pupils. He, like the rest of them, was dressed in a luminous armour of shining plate, that covered him from shin to neck, leaving only his hairy arms bare.

"Forgive my zeal, Master." Zadkiel said simply.

"Don't..." began Jack.

Jack was about to stumble through an answer when Ulfner cut him off, pulling him swiftly on to the next Angel, an equally huge being with flame-red hair and piercing red eyes.

"This is their fine leader the mighty Metatron, Guardian of the Seal."

Metatron closed his eyes and nodded, Jack felt a tremendous rush of warmth and wellbeing as a deep gravelly voice sounded in his head.

"Well met young master."

Jack was hastily introduced to each of the other eight in turn: Sandalphon, Uriel, Raphael, Jophiel, Chamuel, Raziel, Gabriel and the grim faced Michael. All the Angels stood and drew various weapons, raising them in salute; most burned like his with a brilliant light.

Jack lifted his own sword and Ulfner nodded his approval, then a look of terrible sadness crossed his face. All eyes turned to Ulfner as he reached into his robes and pulled out the Necromius Spines, the glowing green glyphs still crawled slowly through the metal.

Silence descended.

Ulfner dropped his robe and stood naked for a moment, stretching one last time; his joints popping noisily again. Then he climbed onto the table and lay flat.

He turned to Jack and took a deep breath, "Jack you need to do this."

Ulfner handed the spines to Jack; at the touch of the warm metal the words of the binding echoed distantly in his head. Jack suddenly knew what had to be done.

"Hammer." said Jack, the weapon changing instantly to a large silver hand tool.

Jack's heart pounded and his hands shook as he placed the tip of the spine against Ulfner's forehead.

"ATEH." Jack and the Angels spoke the word of power together as he drove the spike home.

Ulfner closed his eyes tightly and hissed with the searing pain, "Be swift Jack, Please."

"MALKUTH." He struck the next quickly, with tears blurring his eyes.

"VE GEBBURAH." Strike.

"VE GEDDULAH." Strike.

"LA OHLAM" Strike.

"AMEN." Strike.

With the final spine hammered into place a loud crack filled the air and a small sphere of golden light slowly formed above Ulfner's body. The spines slowly dissolved into the body and the green glyphs spread out over his skin and in a matter of moments his body was reduced to the bone armour it had been before.

The Angels stood with their weapons still forming a point above the orb. Once again the bones floated in the air, waiting for Jack to approach and receive.

Chapter 14

Abandoned

Belthor stood alone, arms crossed and stony faced, silently watching the very last of the heavy carts rumbling down the ramp onto the eastern bank of the Ulfen.

He had sat through their initial horror and outrage, then their bickering, as one by one each of the Tower Lords decided not to send help Westwards to Ness. They had debated and schemed long into the night, before finally agreeing with Riznar's plan to assist in the building of the wall and the new garrison towns needed at intervals along the thousand-mile riverbank.

Thousands of the common bridge-folk, carrying their treasures, but weighed far heavier with fears, had headed into an uncertain life of upheaval and hardship in the massive tented refugee camps springing up all along the riverside.

Belthor raised his staff and far below each of the gathered Tower Lords raised an arm in answer.

"Lift." He intoned.

The huge drawbridge groaned as it slowly lifted and the tower beneath him shuddered as it finally slammed shut, the empty tower resounded with a hollow boom.

Belthor heaved a sorrowful sigh and gave a last glance at the gathered Lords, before turning and heading for the west bank of the Ulfen.

Walking along the wide bridges, he couldn't help but feel for the thousands of homeless, the dark windows of their empty homes echoed a gloomy sadness.

*

As he arrived at the parapets of the last tower he was astounded to see a single warrior holding the reins of two large horses, waiting for him on the road far below. Belthor's heart lifted and for the first time in many days he smiled. He picked up his pace and hurried down through the tower and across the drawbridge.

Belthor stopped short when he was met by a grim but familiar faced girl. She was dressed in tight-fitting black leather armour, with a scabbard at her hip and a long bow across her back. Her blond hair was cropped short in a boyish style but she was still beautiful.

"Samanthiel," Belthor began, "You cannot…"

She raised her hand and as if from nowhere a slender bladed long-sword appeared, the point held unwaveringly at his throat, "Silence mage!"

"My Father is the Captain…" she began, then swallowed and blinked, "…was the Captain of the Guard, and I have been trained well in the martial arts. I am here to take my revenge on the demon that has slain my Father and Brothers."

Belthor smiled sadly and closed his eyes, he slowly lifted his fingers to the blade and pushed it gently downwards. She lowered it, and with a swift fluid movement, slid the blade into the scabbard.

"I will get the chance to join my family in the afterlife soon, and hopefully help someone in doing so." She added.

Belthor placed a hand on her padded shoulder, "Thank you Samanthiel, may the Great Goddess Danu bless and protect you in these hard days to come."

The blessing shook her and tears sprang to her eyes.

Belthor opened his arms and wrapped her in a warm embrace, she hugged into his barrel chest and cried her eyes out.

He released her holding both shoulders tight and staring her right in the eye.

"Samanthiel, you have taken the first steps on a dreadful path. But it is a path you will not be treading alone, for one way or another, these terrible days of darkness must end soon, and Goddess willing, we will triumph. Now I must end this sad chapter in our civilisation's history and destroy the city of Ulfenspan. I and all the peoples of the West wish to thank you Samanthiel, for standing with us when all your city and the East turned away."

"Sam," she said, "Call me Sam, Belthor."

Pride lit her face as Belthor turned slowly to face the rushing waters. He lifted his staff high into the air and slowly swept it in a wide circle above his head, whispering softly. A small ball of blue light formed above their heads and Sam gave a small gasp.

"Sink." The simple command echoed unnaturally loudly, as the ball flew into the water.

Loud cracks sounded as the waters boiled, and the mighty structure vibrated violently as huge chunks of stone fell from the bridges above, the splashes sending waves rushing over the bank. Belthor and Sam led the horses away, heading quickly from the riverside and up the steep grassy slope to a safer vantage point. The view of the collapsing bridges was both breathtaking and tragic, and Sam gave a small cry of despair as her home vanished beneath the waves.

Finally the towers themselves began to fall, collapsing slowly into the boiling froth, severing the ancient link between the two halves of the country forever.

Belthor turned his back on the river with tears in his eyes and reached for the reins and began leading the horse up the hill towards the west and a future darkened with doubts and sadness.

As the last tower fell the ground began to shake in a massive earthquake, and Belthor had to grip his staff tightly to remain standing.

"No!" He cried, as a howling winds sprang up from the Northwest, filling the skies with pendulous black clouds. He stiffened, feeling a glimpse of the tremendous pain one of his brethren suffered in the distance.

"**LA OLAHM**," The mighty word cracked the skies with terrible lightening as day slowly vanished, transforming into an oppressive overcast gloom.

"For all eternity," Belthor whispered in fear, staggering weakly.

Sam gripped his arm, steadying the old mage.

"One more word of power and you'll be reunited with your family sooner than you might hope," Belthor shouted above the storm.

Sam smiled as the heavens opened and torrential rain began to bucket down, plastering her short hair to her head.

"Come Belthor, we have a few more Demons to slay."

Chapter 15

Crow's Revenge

The sun was setting as a dark storm rolled over the city of Ness. In the middle of the rowan circle Krangresh the Demon lay very still; it lessened the burning pain from the silver chains that bound him securely. From his prone position he glared up in contempt at the silhouette of a single mage standing watch behind a shield of magical totems, charms and talismans carved into a stout wooden palisade, hastily constructed atop the reinforced, but ancient, wall.

The penultimate word of power had just shaken the world and Krangresh knew that dozens of its brethren must now be roaming the earth in a frantic search for a magic user to give them the last word. That final word would break the binding and release the remaining thousands of his kind, and the world would finally be theirs.

Suddenly lightning lit the sky, and from the shadows a figure rose up on the palisade and light glinted from a curved blade that slashed downwards viciously. A rolling crash of thunder drowned out the brief scream as the mage died.

Harry the Crow leapt from the palisade and moved slowly towards the rowan circle. He was burned terribly on his cheeks and forehead and his good eye bulged madly.

"Come...closer..." A soft hissing voice enticed him, but with a conscious effort Crow deliberately stopped at the edge of the circle.

The Demon writhed on the ground, twisting to see the figure standing at the edge of its prison. The two stared at each other for moments before Crow reached out and grasped the rowan branch.

"You will use me and we shall kill my enemy," Crow whispered, before adding "Together."

The Demon's eyes narrowed as he realised what the man before him desired; he wanted revenge, pure and simple.

"Yes…yes…free me and we shall release my brethren and you will experience the revenge you lust after." The Demon's eager voice rose in pitch and volume.

Crow pulled the rowan branch from the ground and snapped it, tossing it over his shoulder before removing the remaining branches one by one.

Krangresh began to struggle with renewed strength and the silver chains began to smoke and sizzle against its skin. Crow stepped deliberately close and placed a leather gloved hand on the monster's forehead pushing it heavily into the earth. Then he pulled the curved blade and rammed it into the Demon's eye socket, right to the hilt.

The silver chains stopped smoking and the sizzle faded. A glowing sphere shot from the Demon into Crow's chest, knocking him backwards into the mud. Krangresh lay there inside the mind of a truly evil man.

Crow felt the presence of the Demon filling him with strength, but also felt his own control fading and the steely grip of the Demon's consciousness forcing him to take the lesser role of a viewing passenger.

Crow leapt agilely to his feet and Krangresh began to giggle. He tittered and laughed like a madman, before leaping up over the wall in a single bound.

*

In Lord Ness's keep Lupin lay on the bed, face down, his wound wrapped in various ointment covered leaves. As he slept, a raven haired warlock worked with energy around him; his black robes flapping as he danced a complex ritual, weaving an intricate web of light and love, balancing the dark taint on his aura with the white light of pure moon-power.

Changelings
Dragons and Demons

The bed was surrounded by various powerful objects of his art: A dark bladed dagger, a bell, a candle, a bowl of salt, a cluster of purple amethyst and a golden goblet.

But as his incantations were drawing to a whispered conclusion, the large bay window shattered inwards, showering the room with lethal shards of glass. The warlock reached for his dagger, crying out in alarm as Crow landed on the carpet, his boots crunching noisily. One huge backhanded swipe sent the man flying against the wall with a thud.

Crow luxuriated in the feelings of power flooding through his body, as the demon leant over the concussed man sniffing for magic. Then he stood straight as a far stronger scent reached his senses. The smell of magic was far stronger on the wounded man lying on the bed.

Krangresh growled as he recognised the Changeling that had captured him, so he stalked over and made to grab him but recoiled in pain as the objects of power burst into life, releasing their burning magical energies against him.

Suddenly the door flew open and several guards froze in the doorway, crying out in horror at the sight of the infamous Crow bending over their Lordship's friend. Crow's head snapped up and his over-wide eye narrowed in rage, he hissed and bared his rotten teeth, cursing them for spoiling his fun, but before the guards could react he snatched the warlock under an unnaturally strong arm and leapt from the high window, vanishing into the night.

Chapter 16

Friends Reunited

Jack stood and slowly reached for the armour, his mouth was dry and he wished he could quench his thirst. As his fingertip touched the breastplate the armour leapt upon him. This time he did not fight it and in moments he was encased and rejoined with Ulfner.

"Thank you for being swift Jack," Ulfner's grateful voice echoed in his head, "Now we must take these Angels home."

Metatron smiled as if hearing the voice, and as one, the Angels sheathed their weapons, and joined hands in a giant chain. Jack took a deep breath as Michael and Metatron lightly placed a huge hand on each shoulder, gripping them gently and completing the circle. Then Jack reached up and gripped the glowing orb.

Instantly the room dissolved into a bright white nothingness. All around him he could hear the cries of laughter and joy from the angels, but it took all his will to keep hold of the sphere, as he felt himself being swept through the light.

*

In a flash he stood in the ruined altar room, half filled with rubble and debris from the collapsed ceiling. Metatron looked at the partially blocked stairway and nodded. Jophiel, Raziel and Uriel leapt into action, attacking and smashing the boulders furiously with huge hammers of light, the intensity of their actions startled Jack, who tried to remain impassive.

Ulfner laughed inside him, "Jack these Angels do nothing by half measures. They will clear that stairway in no time."

Metatron frowned, inhaling deeply then he licked at his red lips, as if he was tasting the air. He gripped the hilt of his sword till his knuckles whitened and fairly shook with rage.

"Many have crossed," his voice boomed angrily, "and only one more part of the Mighty Bind holds the rest at bay."

Jack could feel Ulfner's immediate concern as his body surrendered to the Darkbane's presence.

"Where Metatron?" Ulfner asked urgently with Jack's voice.

Metatron closed his eyes concentrating, the hammering angels ceased their toil in anticipation of his reply.

"Not far…South and West in the deep woods beyond the Giant's Teeth. But I fear the worst for they have the final bind and are set to break it soon."

Jack felt his stomach tighten and his skin tremble with Ulfner's anger for the Demons were now desecrating the earth again and his Goddess would feel the pain of their presence.

The Angels redoubled their efforts and soon the passage was clear and they were ready to ascend. Metatron turned to Jack and bowed low, reaching down and offering his hand.

"Master, may I carry you? Time is of the essence and I fear we will need to be swift."

Jack stepped forwards and the large, red hand closed gently around his waist. Then he has hoisted easily onto one broad shoulder as the Angels started to climb the stair. They took the large steps three at a time jogging easily upwards in complete silence.

After a short while Ulfner whispered in his head, "Jack, when we near the surface, have Metatron set you down and we shall lead the way, you should find it an easy run as the armour will help energise you. After all, it is only fitting that the Chosen one precedes the Angels but remember this one thing:

Stand well back and let the Angels free the Dragons. Do not interfere with this in any way; for it is a time of tremendous importance for the Dragons and Angels alike."

Jack nodded inwardly, glad of the advice.

Suddenly a deafening roar shook the stairwell, followed by another, then an almost continuous cacophony of sound echoed down the stairs.

"Set me down please Metatron." Jack shouted out over the din.

The Angels stopped on the steps, eagerly awaiting the command to proceed.

"I will lead the rest of the way. We shall soon reach the surface and when we do, you shall free the Dragons." Jack tried to sound commanding.

Jack was a bit startled when Metatron burst into wild laughter. He bent down and practically roared, with tears of mirth running freely down his red face.

"Master! We are the Dragons!"

Most of the Angels joined in with the joke, but Michael stood silently, grim as usual.

Jack was confused, *We are the Dragons?* He thought to himself.

"Lead on Jack," Ulfner's voice chuckled in his head.

"Follow." He called, taking the lead and running up the deep, wide steps.

The Angels followed at a respectful distance, and Jack was a little annoyed that some were still laughing behind him.

*

. The roaring Dragons fell instantly silent as Jack emerged into a black night of buffeting winds and freezing rain. He stepped aside as Metatron emerged followed closely by Michael and the rest of the large Angels. They formed a semicircle around Metatron as he silently faced the similar arc of Dragons. Red stomped forwards and roared his joy into the storm. Metatron ran to meet him in the middle of the circle and embrace the Dragon with his huge arms. Then the air around them shimmered and began to glow a deep red, Metatron and the red Dragon melted into each other; two becoming one in a fantastic transformation.

The true Angel now stood slightly smaller than before, but now Metatron was dazzlingly beautiful to behold; a flowing mane of gold fell to his broad shoulders; a smooth, noble brow topped eyes of glowing red, above a straight nose and strong jaw. But now he had a pair of brilliant red feathered wings folded across his broad back and his battered plate armour was replaced with a shimmering chain-mail of silver and he carried a helmet resembling a golden Dragon.

Jack stood in the shadows in awe of the spectacle being played out before him, as one by one each Angel was reunited with their Dragon. Each Angel had identical armour and weapons, but their colourful wings separated them, identifying them. He could feel Ulfner's pride at seeing the Angels finally whole again and he was not surprised to discover that Zadkiel was twinned with the aggressive golden Dragon, seeing now the similarities in each.

"Go Jack, take them into battle." Ulfner urged, "By the Goddess! I wish that I could join you!"

"Can I change into a Dragon whilst wearing this armour?" Jack asked.

"The bones will form any shape you need Jack, so come on! There are Demons loose in this world!" Ulfner's excitement was infectious.

Jack leapt up and the angels gathered close, an air of tranquillity settled on the eyrie and the winds dropped away as he was surrounded by a rainbow of wings.

"We must go South, to the city of Ness, there are many people there. That this is where we will stand against these Demons." Jack readied himself for the change.

Metatron gave him a dazzling toothy smile, "Master, I vow that we will not merely stand with you against them, we shall help you smite them from this world forever."

Chapter 17

The Final Bound

Belthor rode towards Ness, it had been transformed into a city preparing for war; hundreds of craftsmen, soldiers and city folk worked tirelessly at the walls, hastily shoring up the collapsed sections, and at digging a deep trench lined with stout wooden stakes before the Northern wall.

Sam was at his side, staring at everything in child-like wonder. She had told him on the journey that this was her first visit to a real city; never having left Ulfenspan in all her sixteen years. Belthor was continually amazed by the girl; sometimes she seemed vulnerable and innocent, but the opposite was obvious when she trained with her sword. He had marvelled at her skill with the blade as she practiced intricate sword-dances against imaginary enemies, every time they stopped on the two day trip.

"You know," she said, "It's funny, but I miss the roar of the water. It is just too quiet on the land."

Belthor laughed, remembering the first time he had crossed the river Ulfen; the rushing waters far below had made him dizzy.

They approached the Northern gate and were met by Lord Ness, his red overcoat was replaced by a shining breastplate of silver-steel and mail leggings, his purple cape was still tied at his shoulders. His long braids were tied at the back in a thick ponytail, which hung over a huge scabbard, tied across his back.

Belthor climbed down from his horse, saddle sore and stiffer than usual. Ness grabbed him in a tight hug, before gripping his long beard and kissing his cheeks.

"Danu be praised!" Ness exclaimed, "You have returned!"

"That is obvious Ness."

"What news from the Council?" asked Ness.

Sam sat quietly as the old friends reunited.

"We are alone, cut-off from the East. The Ulfen flows uncrossed and uncrossable." said Belthor.

Ness's smile faded as fast as it had appeared, the colour draining from his face. "What?" he said.

"Our old adversary Riznar now has his wish, Ness. Ulfenspan is no more."

A chill swept down Sam's spine at Belthor's words. She would never see her home again. A similar chill swept down Ness's spine as he realised that the armies and mages of the East would not be coming to their aid in the days to come.

Belthor nodded, "Samanthiel is the only volunteer from the East to cross and offer aid."

Ness turned to her and bowed low, Sam flushed with shame at her city's inaction, but leapt nimbly to the ground and shook his hand.

"I would beg that both of you keep the lack of aid from the troops and people of Ness for I fear a full scale riot." Then Ness added "Forgive my ill manners my lady, my people and I thank you, Samanthiel."

"I would have sought these demons wherever they were, my Lord. But I am glad I have managed to see a real city before I pass on to the afterlife, to be reunited with my family." she said.

Ness took a sharp intake of breath, "Belthor, I think that you had better come to the keep. Lupin needs your help."

*

Belthor sat at the side of Lupin's bed, head bowed in prayer; building energy. Sam winced as she looked down at the broad back, sliced from the shoulder to near the waist in a horrible gash; inflamed red and weeping a stinking pus. The healing balms and herbs had failed to cleanse the poison from the wound and it would take a far greater healing skill to get him back on his feet.

This is the deadly work of just one demon, was this the same beast that had killed my family? She thought to herself.

Sam gripped the hilt of her sword till her white knuckles hurt; the anger made her feel sick, she knew that before she died, she would try and take many of these monsters with her.

Belthor stood and waved his staff in a slow circle above the bed, whispering softly, before resting it against the bed. Then he placed a crooked hand over the wound and on the bed Lupin moaned in pain. After a moment his arm began to tremble and sweat sprang from his brow. A faint glow surrounded his fingers as energy flowed. On the bed Lupin arched his back, raising his head from the pillow and let out a keening howl, so loud and piercing that the repaired window cracked. Black blood and yellow pus bubbled from the wound, staining the sheets as the poison was purged from his body.

Belthor reached into the wound and gently removed a small piece of hook, it made his bloodied fingertips sizzle as it burned. He carefully placed the Demon flesh on a dish filled with holy water from the temple, where it fizzed and dwindled till nothing remained but a layer of dirt on the bottom of the glass. He then resumed his healing work, flooding Lupin with vital energies.

Belthor kept his hand steady as thick dark hairs suddenly sprouted and moulted in seconds, bones snapped and reformed then snapped again as the change came upon him, then back again in moments. Lupin's cries were painfully loud, as wave after wave of pain wracked his body.

Sam clamped her palms over her ears, yet she was unable to tear her gaze from the agony the man was going through.

"FATHER!" Lupin screamed before collapsing exhausted onto the damp sheets.

Belthor panted near to collapse himself, before slowly removing his shaking hand; the wound was cleaned and closed; nothing remained but a thick white scar. Sam rushed to his side and helped the old man into a nearby chair, he was mentally and physically exhausted.

"Thank you Sam." He managed before falling asleep.

She pushed a small cushion behind his head as he began to snore loudly. On the bed Lupin also began to snore and Sam laughed to herself.

"The Father is so like the Son." Sam whispered.

The door opened and Lord Ness let himself in quietly.

"I knew that he would need greater healing than we could give, but we managed to keep him from deteriorating till Belthor arrived." He said wringing out a large sponge into a bowl of fresh water.

As Lord Ness wiped the tainted blood and pus from Lupin's back and sides, Sam marvelled at a Lord carrying out such a menial task with so much care.

Ness turned and gave her a small smile, answering her unasked question "I would do this for any under my roof, besides Belthor and his kin are almost family to me."

Sam was about to reply when a tremor shook the castle. It grew in intensity to a full quake, and a furious roaring wind sprang up from nowhere.

Belthor leapt from his slumber with a mournful cry, and on the bed Lupin woke and sat bolt upright; eyes wide in fear and panting heavily as if he had just woken from a terrible nightmare.

"**AMEN…**" The word blasted through the world, into the ether and shattered the last of the bindings.

Ness and Belthor looked at each other. Then Belthor took a deep shuddering breath, before nodding, "That is it old friend, they are freed."

Chapter 18

Final Preparations

The heavy wooden door splintered and crashed from its hinges as the Demons spewed forth into the weak, storm-washed morning sunlight. First came dozens, then hundreds that very quickly became thousands of monsters; the smallest and slowest were crushed and trampled into the dead earth by quicker and larger Demons.

Soon a writhing mass of horrible creatures milled around in the dying forest around the dark tower. The grunts and growls turned to screams and cries of weird adulation, as the possessed Lailoken climbed onto the flat roof and raised his thin arms. At his side stood the possessed Crow grinned, displaying a mouthful of rotten teeth. His right hand had been transformed into a long, wicked curved blade, still dripping red.

"Master!" They howled repeatedly.

"Brethren…" Lailoken boomed and waited till the frenzied masses settled slightly, "We shall devour this world…slowly, and this time there will be no hindrance from the detestable Ulfner and his accursed Angels! …Behold."

Lailoken lowered his arms, palms apart, and curled his fingers into claws before him. He opened his mouth impossibly wide and retched noisily, the steaming stream of black vomit formed a large ball, which floated in the air between his hands. He uttered a screeching sound that no human throat should have been able and the black ball floated forwards, above the black masses.

He wiped the slime from his chin and shouted, "This sphere will fly to our first feeding ground, the humans tend to gather in large groups," he chuckled, "Follow it and feed!"

Lailoken's demonic voice was drowned out by a huge roar of approval as the swirling black sphere began to move swiftly South-eastwards.

*

Belthor and Sam walked a double field length from the city, towing a horse and cart in the afternoon sun. He reached into a large crate and began hammering iron rods deep into the tilled earth. The blacksmiths of Ness had been working hammer and tongs, night and day, creating hundreds of the simple metal stakes. The witches and priests had blessed each one, anointing them with the twin powers of the moon and sun.

He moved parallel to the North wall, placing the metal stakes every cart length. Every time he pushed one into the cold soil, he called on his Goddess Danu to imbue them with the protection of fire and ice, so that as he left each one, it glowed red and blue alternately, the colours spread through the earth like spilled ink on parchment, soaking into the ground.

They continued placing rods all long the North and West side of the city in a wide arc. Suddenly Belthor stood straight and cried out in pain.

Sam rushed to his side, "Belthor! What is it?"

"I feel them…" he gasped, swallowing hard, his face screwed up and spat as if he had a bad taste in his mouth.

"Soon," he panted drawing a haggard breath, "They will be here soon Sam. By sunset…tonight."

"Let them come," she said flashing her gritted teeth.

In her mind's eye she could almost see her family waiting on the banks of the celestial river, that flowed through the afterlife, urging her on to a glorious death in the name of their revenge.

Sam looked off to the Northwest and shielded her eyes against the light, something was coming alright but it was in the sky now; a huge black mass speeding towards them. Sam gasped as she realised that it was birds, millions of them, blotting out the light. They flew together in a mass migration, hawks alongside tiny songbirds, every species together.

Belthor quickly pulled Sam towards the cart, "Jump up Sam, I think we are going to have company."

The long grass at the edge of the field became coated in an undulating carpet of creatures, rats and mice ran with stoats and weasels, followed closely by smaller vermin. The air was filled with their high pitched panic as they swarmed past the cart and vanished around the city walls and off to the south.

Then a low rumble shook the nearby tree-line, as a stampede of larger animals broke through, mountain-lions and goats ran beside great horned stags and wild boars; hunters and their usual prey united in their desire to flee before the encroaching doom. Every kind of creature from the woods, hills and mountains fled past the city and onwards to the South and the relative safety of distance.

Sam and Belthor gripped each other for balance and watched as their cart was buffeted and rocked by the terrified stampede. The thunder of their passing and raw odour of fear, assaulted their senses, till the dust settled. Sam remained speechless even after the animals had faded back into the distant southern forest.

"Come Sam, we'd better make haste." Belthor said climbing down.

They continued placing the rods, in a second arc closer to the city, till the sun crossed the sky and the began to slowly settle on the distant hilltops.

*

The sunset was breathtaking; burnishing the deep blue sky with clouds of fire. Belthor stood in the field, next to Lupin and Ness, in the middle of the gathered units of guards. Sam waited with them, her sword sheathed, eyes scanning the distant trees. She averted her eyes bashfully as Lupin stripped, she knew he was a Changeling, but had never witnessed a complete change before, and her curiosity got the better of her.

Lupin called out his words and the guards around about widened into a fearful circle as the change swept over him. Sam peered past the men at the shape twisting on the earth. Loud cracks and growls filled the evening sky and soon a huge, black wolf stood where the man had been.

Sam took a deep breath as Lupin padded silently over to her and looked deep into her soul with his lime green eyes.

"Thank you for helping my Father Samanthiel." His voice echoed into her mind.

"I...I didn't do much..." She stammered breathlessly, flushing.

"Samanthiel, you should not harbour such hatred in your heart, it hangs like a dark shadow over your soul." Sam was about to reply when he continued, "Just remember this: Your kin will be waiting when you pass, whether it is today or in seventy years from now. You do not need to fight today...but if you have chosen your path then I will be honoured to fight alongside you this day."

Sam smiled with tears in her eyes, and hugged Lupin's shaggy neck, "I will be standing here with the *real* people of this land."

Suddenly the trees in the distance began to sway violently, though no wind blew. Then the thrashing stopped and every leaf fell from every tree, as if they had given up hope and surrendered to the swiftly approaching death.

Lord Ness and Sam drew on their blades together, as a hush descended on the guards.

"Here they come." Belthor growled unnecessarily.

Chapter 19

Northern Lights

In the twilight the spreading line of Demons appeared, shining and black like hot tar, as they swarmed over the land. Sensing the closeness of the city, and food, they had crashed through the forest, overtaking the magical ball of vomit and broke into headlong run when they cleared the trees.

But as the fastest hit the line of buried iron, the rods flashed dazzling white, freezing them solid then turned a deep red as flames consumed the frozen monsters; most fell back and rolled around on the ground, losing limbs to the flames, but a few made it through, only to find themselves trapped between two lines of unbearable pain.

The next wave of Demons stopped short of the line, and waited patiently for their master to arrive.

*

Bright stars began to prickle the clear darkness and the full moon crested the hilltops. A long piercing howl cut through the savage noise of the gathering demons. Lupin's heightened senses tingled with joy, and he answered with a keening cry of his own. From off to the South swarmed hundreds of wolves, running in a huge yapping pack, gathering on the left flank of the human defenders.

Lupin sped across and joined his brothers and sisters.

"We could not turn our tails and flee Manwolf." The white wolf greeted him with the simple explanation.

"It warms my heart to have you here brother." Lupin said, lowering his head in a mark of respect for the older wolf.

The old wolf looked up at the moon, "It is good that our bright Sister will be watching over us on this night of nights."

*

The gathered Demons parted and retreated slightly as Lailoken approached the magical defences, with the possessed Crow close behind. He began to laugh as he spotted the iron spikes and his charred brethren. Slowly he moved Lailoken's hand towards the spike, and it glowed softly; but not as bright as when the demons had tried to cross.

"Pathetic," he muttered.

*

Belthor gasped in pain as Lailoken came into view. In his heart he knew that it was not his son pulling at the iron spike, but he felt terrible for him all the same, for the flesh of his hands were being repeatedly frozen and burned, as he finally managed to wrestle the spike from ground.

All along the line, the flashing dimmed slightly, then Crow joined in and the pair began ripping the defences apart. A feeling of sickness and dread swept over the defenders; as the demonic influences grew with each pin pulled. The lines wavered and a few defenders turned and fled into the city.

"Steady!" Roared Ness.

The Northern lights began to appear, painting the clear dark with swirling colours. Belthor and the people of Ness looked skywards as, what appeared to be shooting stars, sped through the night; but these were celestial bodies of a different kind.

A piercing screech split the sky and a burst of flames lit the growing darkness as a huge armoured dragon flew among the stars, its roar drowning out the tumultuous Demons.

*

Jack swooped from on high, roaring with all his strength, Ulfner's armour now coated his scales with glowing green runes that gave him the energy required for the arduous flight.

The Angels flew around him in a swirl of colour, their wings staining the sky. A fierce light glowed around their heads, illuminating their grim faces and glistening from their armour and weapons, as they sped through the night.

In Jack's head Ulfner whooped and laughed joyously as they flew, for in the distance the line of lights around the city had dimmed, yet were still lit. As the abominable horde came into sight, Jack could feel an intense heat radiating from the Angels. Their rage was a racing pulse, which grew with every beat of their mighty wings.

*

Belthor fell to his knees and wept as Jack landed with the Angels. Sam stood with her mouth hanging open in awe as the radiant beings formed a line between them and the Demons. Ness placed a hand on Belthor's shoulder and helped him to his feet.

"Jack!" Belthor cried.

Jack tore his smouldering eyes from the Demons and swung his head around and down towards the shout.

Ulfner took control of Jack's body and made him lower his head to the ground, facing the old man.

"Change me." Ulfner's words were filled with a tremendous power, and in a burning moment of agony Jack stood as a boy once more, still encased in the glowing bones.

He was bewildered and angry for he wanted nothing more than to smash and burn the Demons, and he rebelled against the presence in his mind, but Ulfner had a greater purpose for his body.

"Jack, please let me do this."

Once again Ulfner controlled the lad.

"Sword" he said.

The flaming blade sprang from nowhere, and he preceded to thrust it deep into the earth. He pushed it till the last quarter of the blade and the crossed hilt remained. The defenders began muttering, but Belthor held up a hand and with a magical gesture silenced them all.

As one, the Angels drew upon their weapons.

*

Crow gave a low throaty grunt as he heaved at the burning iron, but he stopped pulling on his spike and watched as the Angels across the field stabbed their weapons into the earth. These Angels were different; smaller, brighter and they had wings; but he knew that they were not invincible, the thousands of years fighting them in the Netherworld had taught him that much.

"Come brethren," Zarakigesh cried as the lights in the ground finally died, "Tonight you will feast on Angel flesh."

As one, the demons swept forward.

*

Ulfner made Jack touch the top of the hilt and cry, "**ATEH**."

Then he bent and placed a palm downwards on the earth, "**MALKUTH**."

He touched the right edge of the sword's cross hilt, "**VE GEBBURAH**."

He touched the left edge, "**VE GEDDULAH**"

Then he placed his hand on his heart and cried, "**LA OHLAM**."

Before finally shouting to the stars, "**AMEN**."

A low rumble shook the earth as a mound seemed to grow and swell in the field.

The Angels pulled their swords from the ground and pointed at the hillock and light from their blades lanced into the land. The earth erupted in an explosion of dirt, but it did not fall, for the rocks and earth formed a gigantic being that dwarfed even the mighty Angels.

Jack and the Angels fell to their knees before their Goddess Danu; a shimmering vortex of swirling rock and lightning; beautifully elemental and terribly powerful.

Chapter 20

Danu

The Goddess turned her stony gaze on the approaching Demons and lifted one mighty arm of rock and lightning.

"Stop," Danu's voice thundered.

Instantly the demons froze, transforming into a sea of dark statues in the moonlight. A hush fell upon the world and every living thing listened as she spoke in a slow sad voice.

"These are terrible times...Demons once again sweep my lands with impunity, whilst man has abandoned their fellow man in their darkest of hours. But...these times will pass – as they always pass - and balance will be restored."

Her glowing eyes flashed brighter, as she continued, "From this moment, and forever more you Demons will enter the circle of life. You will live and die and be reborn, without the dark influences that taints and devours life."

With a flick of her rocky wrist a huge flash lit the night and a visible darkness rose from the still monsters. It hovered, a swirling cloud of evil magic before dissipating on the cleansing winds.

Danu turned slowly and looked down upon the defenders and the line of Angels, "I will not destroy these Demons for you, humans, the balance must be restored by your own hand. Do not fear them overly, for their powers of possession have been dispelled, but do not forget that their physical strength and skills still remain."

The Angels rose, spreading their wings wide and sheathing their weapons in unison.

Her tone softened slightly as she reached down and swept her glowing hand along the Angel's wingtips, "My Angels, you shall aid these humans in their struggle against these creatures of darkness till the sun's light spills across this field; only then you shall rejoin me in the astral realms; whatever the outcome of this night."

For the first time since the Netherworld was created the grim Angel Michael smiled.

Then the Goddess turned her hot gaze on Jack.

"Jack the Changeling and Ulfner Darkbane, two champions in one small frame. Approach me Jack."

Jack crossed the field, passing between Metatron and Gabriel, and stopped before the Goddess, his heart racing. Danu held out her left palm and spat a ball of light into her huge hand, mixed it with earth, and then formed it into a crude clay golem. Then she reached down and swept Jack up in her right hand and lifted him to her face and inhaling deeply.

"Farewell Jack…" Ulfner's voice faded in his mind.

Slowly the green runes faded from the bone armour and Jack could feel Ulfner's soul moving, it left him feeling strangely empty inside. Then she exhaled over the creation in her other hand and the green runes appeared in the twitching clay.

A ball of light formed around the figure, which quickly faded to reveal Ulfner Darkbane remade and alive, resplendent in shining armour and sporting a glowing pair of golden wings. She lowered him to the ground and placed Jack at his side.

"Ulfner, join your Angels."

Ulfner bowed low, gave Jack a nod and promptly marched back to the lines. Danu gazed at Jack; swirling tingles of energy circulated from his skull down his spine and a feeling of warmth and gratitude filled him

"Jack, from this day forth the change will not be detrimental to your health, or that of your family."

"My family?"

Jack could sense her benevolent smile.

"Yes Jack, I will remove the toll from all your family here on the field and those elsewhere. The gathered seasons will fall from them, and time will progress naturally for them all till the day they die; whichever shape they choose to assume. Now go and join your people and prepare for battle."

Jack felt dizzy with the revelations and turned in turmoil, leaving the Goddess slowly sinking back into the earth.

*

The Master controlling Lailoken knew that the demons were going to struggle; for he had directed their battles in the Netherworld using the dark magic; overcoming their fears and controlling their mindless rage. Now the Angels stood like a fiery wall of light that hurt his host's eyes, and the immense power radiating from them made the small hairs stand all over his body.

This was the first time that they faced their ancient adversaries without magic, and knowing the struggle Krangresh had endured retrieving the last warlock, he began to feel unsettled; something akin to fear.

Even though he felt tremendous rage at the loss of his dark magic, he was clever enough to know that his host Lailoken was a powerful mage, and he could use that power to flee.

There will be other ways to take my revenge, he thought to himself.

As the Goddess finally sank beneath the earth, the effect of her magic slowly wore off.

Lailoken straightened in the moonlight, glaring at the glowing barrier of colourful Angels before the people of Ness. Crow growled at his side, drawing upon his dagger with his left hand and raising his bladed right hand.

"Slay them all, and feast upon their flesh!" he roared, and waited as his brethren rushed past in attack.

Then in the chaos he called upon the change buried deep in Lailoken's mind.

"With talons sharp, and wings so strong, In the skies, I now belong."

Lailoken's body hunched as the Demons streamed by on either side, he tore the cloak from his body as large brown feathers began to sprout. His cry of pain transformed to the screech of a large eagle.

*

Belthor was a changed man; his white beard was now fuller and shot through with black. His shoulders were larger and heavily muscled, and the weariness that had weighed him for so long was now gone, now he stood straight and tall. As the Demons surged forward, he flexed his muscles and dropped the cloak from his back and let out a deep growl.

"I bear the sorrow, I bear the pain, let me become a bear again."

He spread his arms wide, accidentally knocking Lord Ness backwards slightly; they thickened sprouting thick brown fur. Moments later a massive brown bear stood amidst the tensed defenders, rising high on two clawed feet. Belthor roared into the night as a silhouette of an eagle passed the moon.

*

Jack joined the lines of defenders, calling upon his sword as he desperately sought Belthor and Lupin amongst them.

"To me Jack!" Lord Ness called him as the Demons began to move.

Jack was astonished that the Lord even knew his name, he had seen him in the past certainly, but always from a distance and always surrounded by guards.

Lord Ness nodded to Ulfner and the Angels, a grim smile on his face.

"Men of Ness! Your families have fled this city and are safe for the time being, but these monsters will hunt them down and kill every last one, unless we stop them this night. You have heard the words of Danu, your Goddess! Tonight we will punish these Demons for the harm they have done her, and the harm they intend us all...Men of Ness ..." He cried with passion, " Men of Ness, Charge!"

Above their heads, on the rebuilt walls, archers loosed volley after volley of arrows high into the air, falling in a deadly rain into the middle of the surging Demons.

*

Ulfner raised his arm in a silent command. As one he and the Angels swept across the fields to meet the Demon army head on in an explosion of light, their weapons sweeping, decimating the front ranks. Then, after the initial assault, they leapt into flight and swooped gracefully upwards and dived in a rainbow arc to attack the Demon's left flank repeatedly.

*

"By the light of our sky-sister and in the name of the Earth Mother…" Lupin howled to the brothers and sisters of the pack, "…Make them pay dearly for every step they take on this field this night." Lupin and the wolves bounded forwards and attacked the Demon's right flank in a frothing fury of howling attack and retreat, causing light casualties, but heavy confusion.

*

Ness led the men in a charging frontal assault, shields locked and spears thrusting, scything the first Demons and advancing over their fallen bodies. Then with a mighty clash the main body of the Demons smashed into them. The line buckled under the ferocious assault, then broke. The men cast their spears and drew upon their short swords, while their comrades in the second and third ranks continued stabbing and slicing over the shoulders of the fiercely battling front rank.

Amid the chaos and clamour of battle a slight figure danced among the Demons, her long silver sword dealing death on every side.

Sam laughed uncontrollably as she cut and thrust, the sound of her voice drowning out the cries and screams of the wounded and dying. Every second stretched into long moments as the monsters seemed to melt before her fury; though each Demon that fell did nothing to salve the pain in her heart.

Suddenly she staggered backwards and tripped over a fallen Demon, her small shield shattered by the heavy blow of a spiked club, wielded by a huge screeching monster. It advanced amazingly swiftly for a beast of its size, the weapon held high ready to pummel her to death.

"Spear!" Jack's voice rang out over the battle, as his flaming weapon lanced through the demon's throat, killing it slowly in a shower of black blood.

Sam leapt to her feet and discarded the now useless shield, and was amazed to see a figure in strange bone armour wading into the fray beside her.

Jack flashed her a grim smile, "Sword!" He cried and slashed another beast. They fought side by side, advancing into the hellish mayhem, swords whistling together.

"Face me Hawk!" An ungodly voice roared above the din of battle.

Jack paused for a moment and his blood ran cold, there, amidst the bulging eyes and gnashing teeth, stood his old enemy Crow, horribly disfigured by fire and the Demon using his body.

Crow leapt agilely over the female warrior that tried to block his path, slashing out with his dagger, aiming to cut at her throat.

She was quicker though, Sam ducked and the blade clattered off her helmet; knocking her to the ground.

"Whip," said Jack, his voice calm, whilst his stomach turned somersaults.

As Crow landed before him, he lashed out with the whip, cracking the dagger from his blackened hand.

Krangresh - the Demon in Crow - roared with frustrated rage and swept up his bladed right hand, and spat "You will not be able to take this blade so easily, Changeling."

"Be still Demon!" Crow struggled momentarily with the Demon for mastery over his body.

Jack took his advantage, launching a ferocious attack, but each blow was parried and countered too easily and without Ulfner's aid he was no match for the monster. Jack's sword skill was certainly improved by the magical weapon, but Crow had spent a lifetime in the gutters of Ness; winning all his knife fights, and his Demon had spent aeons fighting the Angels in the Netherworld. A few moments of slash and parry and Jack was caught with a ferocious punch to his face that sent him flying. He landed in the mud stunned, tears springing unbidden.

Crow laughed hideously and raised his blade to finish the lad, when a huge black wolf leapt through the air, his jaws snapping the wrist and severing the bladed limb. Crow's eyes widened in pain and fear as a razor-sharp blade suddenly burst from his chest, thrust savagely by the forgotten female. His slavering mouth opened and closed in a gurgling cry as the blade was twisted and pulled swiftly clear. Then a huge roar rumbled from behind and a gigantic brown bear caught him in a mighty hug, the crunching and splintering of the bone was audible over the tumult of the battle. The crushed, lifeless body was tossed easily aside as Belthor the bear towered over Jack.

"Change Jack! Join your family!"

Chapter 21

Battle

Jack writhed on the blood soaked earth; overtaken by the change. Around him a strange trio of sentries stood firm in the raging tide of battle: a bear, a wolf and a grim-faced girl. Any demon that dared come within range of the blade, tooth or claw was hacked and torn limb-from-limb in their combined defence.

*

The human defenders were almost overwhelmed by the surging demons, but the archers loosed the last of their arrows and leapt from the walls, drawing on their swords and rushing to bolster the wavering defenders.

Suddenly a widening circle of space appeared amid the chaos of the battlefield as Jack rose in his full Dragon form, wings spread to the maximum and roaring thunderously. The Demons scattered in all directions as Jack loosed a rolling ball of flame into the main body of the advancing horde. The battle ceased momentarily as every eye turned on him and the sky was cloaked with billowing smoke and sparks of the burning Demons.

Jack lashed out with every weapon he had been blessed with, roaring with joy and rage in equal measure, luxuriating in his power as he swiped dozens with his barbed tail. He rose to full height as several demons tried to leap upon his back, these he picked off easily with his teeth, giving them a crunch before tossing them far with a flick of his serpentine neck. Dozens more perished under his foot and claw, before he took to the air, swooping high and circling the field.

A dreadful sinking feeling filled his several dragonish stomachs as the enormity of the task they faced became apparent; countless thousands still flooded onto the field, all bent on the destruction of every living thing. From his high vantage and with his perfect night vision, Jack easily picked out Belthor, Lupin and the girl fighting their way back towards the city.

"My family..." He thought to himself in desperation, diving to their aid.

He raked the ground at high speed, his razor talons tearing and ripping a pathway through the pressing mass of Demons, before he swooped back into the air, roaring with exhilaration. As he flew Jack could feel the seething hatred of the Demons, but he could also feel a new emotion radiating from them - fear.

Coming to a hover, Jack could see the first glimmering of light in the east and a desperate fear swept through him.

"Jack!" Ulfner's voice boomed into his mind.

Jack was suddenly aware that Ulfner and the Angels now surrounded him in a hovering circle of light.

"Jack our time here is short. Prepare yourself to receive our last gift." Ulfner smiled, his black eyes glittering in the moonlight, and flew close to Jack's huge scaly head and placed a glowing hand upon his horned snout.

Jack felt something begin to grow inside him, as one by one, each Angel placed a burning hand upon his scales. His breathing slowed and deepened as his awareness expanded. He felt a tremendous power flowing through his veins, each heartbeat increasing the surging energy. His bones seemed to vibrate and twist under his thick skin till Jack thought he would explode. Then in one exhalation, he poured liquid flame into an almighty floating fireball. Jack struggled with his newly acquired power to hold the sun-like ball aloft as it grew in size, before dropping it directly onto the centre of the monstrous gathering.

Thousands perished in moments in the unnaturally hot inferno, incinerated instantly as the earth burned in a wide circle, turning the field into a demonic charnel house. Hundreds of surviving Demons, still arriving on the field, turned-tail and fled in terror back into the forest.

Jack and the Angels fell, exhausted, from the sky, landing heavily in the smouldering ashes.

*

A small pocket of Demons still fought with the wolves, and several still raged against the defenders, but these were swiftly overwhelmed and finally destroyed.

A strong wind picked up from the South and blew away the terrible stench of charred Demon, and when the smoke cleared, the aftermath of the battle finally became apparent. Hundreds of defenders were dead or grievously injured, but on the other side of the coin, many thousands of demons had now joined the circle of life as the Great Goddess Danu had promised them.

*

Lupin bounded across the burned wasteland and joined the surviving wolves. The old white wolf lay flat on his side upon the earth, his muzzle and neck was matted and black with Demon blood, and as he panted heavily, bright blood coloured the froth on his black lips. Lupin gave a low whine of sadness and nuzzled his old friend.

"I will suffer for long hours yet Manwolf...please...end it with our Sister's blessing."

Around them the gathered wolves all began to sing to their bright sister in the sky; songs of loss and sadness; songs of valour and courage; songs for their fallen brothers and sisters to follow into the night; on their way to the great hunt among the stars.

Lupin ceased his song and swallowed hard.

*

Lord Ness co-ordinated his medical teams, tending to the wounded himself alongside the healers and doctors, his own injuries ignored over the wellbeing of his people. Belthor and Ulfner carried Jack to the gates and laid him gently on the dew-covered grass. The bodies of the Angels lay nearby; the glow now gone from their wings, empty vessels cracked and broken, their liquid life drained and finally moved on to join their Goddess.

Jack was unconscious; his dragon form had suffered severe injuries, which had transferred to his human body when he hit the ground. Belthor knelt at his feet summoning up healing power, while Ulfner knelt at his head with one hand on his brow, murmuring softly. Jack took a deep breath and a shadow of pain crossed his young face, slowly his eyelids fluttered open.

Belthor stood, staggered and gave a great cry of relief and then collapsed in exhaustion.

*

Ulfner stood gazing into the lightening sky. A shuddering breath interrupted his solemn reverie.

"Are you injured Samanthiel?" He asked quietly, approaching her from behind.

Sam sat, sobbing softly, on a rock near the gates, her battered body throbbing with tired pain, and her discarded sword lying carelessly across her mud-caked boots.

She turned and shook her head, her filthy face streaked clean with tear tracks, "I am fine, my Lord, it saddens me to see the sacrifice that these noble beings made, whilst I was unable to do the same."

Ulfner smiled sadly, "Do not grieve for them Samanthiel, we were sent here to help mankind, predestined in ages past by fickle fates. Your destiny was not to end here this day. You will go on and do great things with your life, you will make new friends, you will travel great distances and see amazing wonders, and yes you will get the chance to help these people. You will help them rid the planet of the Demon scourge."

Ulfner placed a large hand upon her padded shoulder, the feelings of sadness and pain were lessened as a radiant image of the Angel Michael appeared before her shimmering in the dawn's weak light.

Michael smiled and drew his huge fiery blade, then turned and offered her the hilt, "Samanthiel, take this, my blade - Nemesis, it has served me well in more battles than I care to remember. May it bring you the strength and courage you need in the times to come."

Sam stood on shaky legs and took a firm grip of the offered hilt. The surprisingly light sword pulsed in her hands, vibrating with alien energies. Right before her eyes the blade shrank remoulding itself into the familiar shape of her own sword. Stunned, she reached for her own weapon, then she remembered it lay carelessly at her feet. Sam turned ready to retrieve the scabbard, but nearly collapsed in fright as she faced her own body, still sitting on the stone, eyes closed, the Angelic Ulfner standing with a hand still on her shoulder. Sam's mouth opened and closed wordlessly, speechless she spun back to face Michael, only to become doubly shocked to find her Father standing there in his place, a shimmering, younger version of the tower captain she knew and loved dearly.

"Sammy...I love you." His words echoed as if he spoke in a great cavern, "I am so proud of you. We all are. In time Sammy, the pain will lessen, you will love and live a happy life...with our blessings. Farewell my little princess..."Tears sprang into Sam's eyes as her ghostly father slowly began to fade.

"Daddy!" She cried, "Daddy I love you..."

The fading figure smiled and raised a hand in recognition before finally disappearing. A tingling rush seemed to pull at the centre of her back, and in an instant her spirit jumped back into her living body.

"Samathiel...are you well?" said Ulfner.

Sam stood and picked up her discarded sword. She studied it closely, it seemed to be the same weapon, but now the blade was intricately engraved with the image of a dragon on one side and an Angel on the other.

Chapter22

Epilogue

Ulfner stood with Belthor watching the sun's tip creep over the hilltop into a pale red sky.

"I can remove the pain in your heart Belthor." Ulfner made to place a healing hand upon Belthor's shoulder.

"No. Please do not," cried Belthor, "It reminds me of my quest. The pain I feel will be nothing compared to the horror my son, Lailoken, is enduring in the hands of that demon."

"You face a tenacious adversary, powerful and deadly. He will not be easy to defeat alone." Ulfner closed his eyes for a moment, he murmered to himself as if conversing with someone, before opening his eyes again, "Raziel - the keeper of wisdom and lore - has written a tome, in it is written all knowledge of the hidden arts. It would prove most useful if only you could find it…"

Suddenly he stopped, as if he had divulged too much. Belthor was about to ask about the book, when Ulfner raised a halting hand.

"It is time Belthor, the Lord our Sun is waking from his slumber, his rays will feed new energy into this blighted land and balance will be restored."

As the light of the sun hit Ulfner's wingtips, they began to slowly dissolve, becoming transparent.

"Belthor…" Ulfner's words echoed through the ether, "…seek your Sister…seek your…Sister."

As the sun finally rose clear of the hills, Ulfner and the Angels vanished completely, leaving a slightly dazed Belthor to contemplate his advice.

With a heavy heart Belthor lifted his cloak over his shoulder and fastened the dragon-shaped silver pin, he turned his gaze to the east; the direction he had seen the eagle take.

"So close Lailoken," he whispered to himself.

"Yes Father, but not close enough."

Belthor's heart leapt and he whipped around catching, the now young, Lupin in his arms, gripping him in a tight hug. He was in his mid twenties, but looked young for his age.

"My elder brother has escaped his judgement. Eastwards, probably over the river."

"Yes I spotted his Eagle form." said Belthor quietly.

"I have a bad feeling about that," Lupin began, "That damnable Demon could easily find allies in the East."

Belthor nodded, "We have more pressing needs at the moment though Lupin. There are the injured, and the remnants of the demon horde, though they have scattered they will plague this region. Trade with the Western City-states will cease and hard times will soon follow."

Lupin knelt beside the make-shift stretcher. Jack lay sleeping, wrapped in a cloak for warmth. He moaned and tried to turn over, but an old leather belt was strapped across his chest, immobilising him.

Jack opened his eyes, squinting against the dawn's light, "Who are you?" He croaked with a parched throat.

"Come on Jack," Lupin laughed good-naturedly, reaching for a small silver flask from his cloak "I haven't changed that much have I?"

He pulled the cork and offered the flask to Jack's cracked lips. A tiny amount of amber liquid poured into his mouth, causing him to cough and splutter painfully before swallowing.

"Lupin? What was that awful stuff? What will I change into this time?" Jack joked.

"You have done well, Nephew. My blood sang with pride when you appeared last night. I told you that you had a family Jack. I just neglected to mention just who the family was." He laughed, " Belthor is your Grandfather and I am your Uncle; your Father's Brother."

"My Father? Is he here? And the girl? Is she my Sister?" Jack managed his eyes darting.

Lupin looked up at Belthor, who had turned away with tears in his eyes.

Sam and appeared at Lupin's shoulder.

"No Jack," Sam began, her eyes filling again, "I am not your Sister, we are not related."

"Then who…" Jack started, a puzzled frown crossing his pale face.

Belthor put his arm around Sam's shoulder, as a single tear ran down her dirty cheek.

"Samanthiel has the courage of a dragon; the speed of a wolf; the strength of a bear; and the grace of an Angel," said Belthor, "She is not a Changeling Jack, but she is blessed all the same and we will welcome her into our new family. As to your Father…just get yourself fit and strong and we shall talk of him later."

Sam looked down at Jack and smiled, her face transformed beautifully as she knelt by Jack's side. She leant close and whispered in his ear, "Get well soon little Brother, for we have many Demons to hunt…"

The End…for now

Read on for a free Chapter from the next book

A preview of

Changelings

Book 2

The Book of Raziel

Changelings

Book 2

The Book of Raziel

Introduction

The young guard rubbed his freezing hands together and attempted to warm his fingers over the glowing coals of the brazier.

"It helps if you stick em behind your breastplate son." The older guard offered, his breath crystallising in the cold night air.

"Cheers." He copied his partner, tucking his hands in behind his thick leather armour, "What about me feet? Mine are like blocks of ice."

The old guard laughed, "Just stamp them lad, or march. But don't let Captain Reed spot you away from the post, or he'll be wearing your guts for garters in the morning."

A deep rumble of thunder interrupted their banter. A puzzled look crossed the older guard's face, for it was a cold cloudless night. The young guard peered around nervously into the gloom; the field was empty except for the massive burial mounds in the distance, the blackened earth dusted with a moon-reflecting sparkle of frost.

"Don't worry lad, there hasn't been a demon sighted for well over a month now. The Captain says they probably wont come back this way, not with them Changelings here."

"You were there, right? At the battle with the demons. They say that the Goddess herself rose from the earth, right over there." He pointed into the darkness.

The older guard nodded solemnly, "I stood with Lord Ness and the Changelings, when young Lord Jack flew from the sky in his dragon form." He began, the young guard hanging on his every word.

"Yep, that was some night. Jack the Changeling swooped down with the Angels just as the demons began to attack. Then the ground shakes and Danu herself rises from the earth, all rocks and fire! She takes away the demons magic and leaves us to fight them…"

"Tell us about the fire!" The young guard interrupted excitedly.

"Give us some peace, you impatient pup." He growled..

"There was thousands of them, boy. All teeth and claws, bloody deadly things they were. But we fought long and hard, musta killed bouta dozen of them myself." The older guard shuddered and pulled his cloak tighter about his shoulders, before continuing in a whisper, "There was just too many of them, too many. I lost loadsa good mates that night, not just soldiers either mind, city folks stood with us. Good men all."

He sniffed his eyes watering with more than the cold night air.

"But Lord Jack and the Angels did something miraculous. Somehow they made a gigantic fireball in the sky, brighter than the midday sun it was, and they just dropped it bang in the middle of the monsters. You should have seen it, the heat was terrible, I lost me damn eyebrows! The surviving demons turned tail and fled. But Lord Jack and the Angels fell, crashed into the ashes. We thought the young Lord was a goner, but he is made of sterner stuff. He was laid up for a few months before him and that warrior girl – Samanthiel - started hunting down the last of the demons."

"Have you seen his bone armour?" The younger guard cut in again, "They say it is the magical bones of Ulfner Darkbane no less!"

"Yep he was wearing it once he changed back into a person. They say that it is indeed Ulfner's bones, gotten from deep within a mountain where the dragons were, way up North in the Giant's Teeth Mountains. No blade can pierce that armour, they say, wouldn't mind some myself." He ended with a wry grin.

Suddenly a flash of lightning burst through the sky and hit one of the distant burial mounds, and in a brief moment the young guard thought he could see a figure appear silhouetted on the smoking hilltop. Both shielded their eyes, their night-vision destroyed by the brightness.

"I think I saw something."

The older guard scowled, "Don't be soft lad, nothing could have survived a lightning strike." He rubbed his sore eyes.

Moments later a soft breath of wind brushed the older guard's cheek, with it a hint of spice. Instinctively he pushed the younger guard to the side and drew his sword.

"*Run boy,* raise the alarm!" he roared.

The younger guard frowned, frightened and confused by his friends sudden action.

A large hooded figure materialised between the guards, dressed in black clothes and cloak, crouching into a deep fighting stance. The young guard stared hypnotically as a long slender blade appeared in the stranger's hand. The old guard licked his lips and lunged. The attack was easily parried and side-stepped. The dark figure lunged quickly past the old guard and reversed the blade, thrusting it swiftly and violently upwards behind him into the guard's back, the fight was over in a few seconds.

The old guard coughed and blood bubbled on his lips as a ragged breath escaped him, and his legs gave way. The dark man cleaned his blade on the old guard's cloak and sheathed his weapon before turning to the lad, who had not run, but stood with his own sword drawn, the point wavering as his arms trembled.

"Count yourself lucky boy, I have not been paid to kill children." He spoke in a well refined, deep voice, "Pity…" He chuckled softly.

He swept forwards and swiftly chopped the lad's neck sharply with his open hand, leaving the unconscious boy slumped on the frozen earth. He reached to a silver eye that hung on a leather thong around his thick neck, and as his fingers touched it he whispered "Dark" and vanished into invisibility.

James A. McVean

Coming Soon

Changelings Book 2 - The Book of Raziel

A wounded Belthor is kidnapped by a mysterious assassin,
Dark treachery rules in the distant capital of Darkhaven,
Jack must confront the Demon possessing his Father.

The Book of Raziel is another fast paced, exciting, fantasy adventure with
Jack the Changeling and his Angelic warrior companion Samanthiel.

*

Gaia's Sword

Snowthorn was a dragon filled with a terrible rage. *They* had
abducted his Father! *They* had murdered his Mother! *They* had torn his
family apart! *They* were the Annunaki - Terrible beings from the distant
planet Nibru, seemingly bent on raping Mother Earth of her natural
resources, desperate for Gold!

But Snowthorn was going to stop them, helped on his virtuous quest
for revenge by his brother and sister. He was trained by the Old Blind
Oracle and magically empowered by the Earth Goddess Gaia, becoming her
champion, her Sword.

Omens are sought and found, and Ancient Prophecies are fulfilled. The
boundary of death would be crossed and conquered.

*

Gaia's Sword is a retelling of the creation mythology on a grand scale. As
seen from the point of view of a Snow Dragon – Snowthorn. Based around the
ancient Mesopotamian Legends of the Annunaki.

I hope you enjoyed this tale. Please feel free to Email me and let me know what you think!!

MCVEANJIM@aol. com